THE BONE SCRAPER LEGACY

GABRIEL FARAGO

This book is brought to you by Bear & King Publishing.

Publishing & Marketing Consultant: Lama Jabr
Website: https://xanapublishingandmarketing.com/
Sydney, Australia

Cover Design by Giovanni Banfi
Image Contributor: Miro - Stock.adobe.com

First published 2024 © Gabriel Farago

ISBN: 978-0-9876283-9-8

Also by Gabriel Farago

Note from the author

Every piece of literature begins with a spark or two of inspiration. Often these sparks are stored away – sometimes for years – in the hidden recesses of our memory before they return unexpectedly and ignite creativity. This was definitely what happened here.

I remember the days and the occasions well. New Zealand is one of my favourite destinations and I visit often, mainly for long hikes through the spectacular mountain wilderness and rainforests on the South Island, to take some time out and recuperate after a long and exhausting period of research and writing.

On this occasion, I spent a few days in Auckland and visited Auckland Art Gallery because there was a special exhibition I wanted to see: the work of Charles Goldie (1870–1947) – one of New Zealand's most prominent painters, best known for his portrayal of Māori dignitaries – was on display.

As soon as I set eyes on the portraits, I was overwhelmed by the emotional impact of the spectacular paintings. One in particular stood out: a stunning portrait of Te Ao Te Rangi Wharepu (1811–1910), a Waikato warrior of the Ngāti Mahuta tribe. What was particularly impressive about the painting was the depiction of the warrior's *moko*, the intricate full-facial tattoo, which was one of the hallmarks of Goldie's work.

The second spark of inspiration was from a photograph I came across several years later, during research for one of my books.

The photograph in question was taken in 1895 and showed Major General Horatio Robley with his macabre collection of *Mokomokai* – mummified, tattooed Māori heads – traded for muskets during the nineteenth-century New Zealand Wars.

The third spark was a book by the Greek–Armenian mystic G.I. Gurdjieff (c. 1866–1949), *Beelzebub's Tales to His Grandson*, one of the most extraordinary and complex books I've ever read and which, according to British poet and literary critic, Martin Seymour-Smith, is one of the most influential books ever written.

The fascinating history surrounding the *Mokomokai* and their bizarre trade became the inspiration for the central storyline, and Goldie's portrait of the Waikato warrior inspired a principal character in the novella: the warrior chief Parema Te Pahau.

Some of the esoteric ideas expressed in Gurdjieff's book have been used to shape Tristan, one of the key characters in *The Jack Rogan Mysteries Series*.

Because accuracy — especially of historical and cultural material — is paramount, I have meticulously researched Māori history and customs in libraries, museums, and galleries, both in Australia and New Zealand, and they have, to the best of my knowledge, been accurately and respectfully presented.

I acknowledge and pay my respects to Aboriginal and Torres Strait Islander peoples as Traditional Owners, Custodians of Country and First Nations in Australia, and to Māori as *tangata whenua* and *te Tiriti o Waitangi* partners in Aotearoa New Zealand.

Gabriel Farago
Leura, Blue Mountains, Australia

Contents

Prologue

The Battle of Wharekauri: 10 October 1840

Ignoring the ominous storm clouds approaching from the north, Parema Te Pahau stared out to sea, his expression stern, his stance defiant. He was preparing himself for what he knew would be a fateful day not only for himself, but also for his *iwi*, his tribe. He lifted his face to greet the sun as it appeared hesitantly out of the morning mist, the first rays illuminating his striking *pūkanohi*, his full-facial tattoo, giving his handsome yet frightening features an almost surreal glow.

The Māori warriors standing respectfully behind him watched in awe as their chief raised his arms and began to chant. He was addressing Tūmatauenga, the god of war, asking for victory. As a revered *tohunga matakite*, not only could Te Pahau foretell the future, but he could also communicate with the gods.

Even in his twilight years, he was an imposing figure, his long hair tied into a traditional knot on top of the head, accentuating his striking *moko*. Tall, powerfully built, with massive arms, and legs like tree trunks, his prowess on the battlefield was legendary, and his cunning battle tactics had led his *iwi* to victory on many occasions.

Five years earlier, Te Pahau had persuaded his *iwi*, Ngāti Mutunga, and their allies, Ngāti Tama, to leave their embattled territory near Wellington and find a new home on Wharekauri, the Chatham Islands.

Conquering and enslaving the docile Moriori, the local natives, had been spectacularly successful, further enhancing Parema Te Pahau's reputation as an outstanding leader and visionary who had the ear of the gods.

However, squabbles over land and slaves between Ngāti Mutunga and Ngāti Tama developed over the years, with younger warriors asserting themselves in the hope of becoming leaders, making it increasingly difficult for Te Pahau to assert his authority.

Matters came to a head when one of his sons was ambushed and killed during a visit to an Ngāti Tama *marae* to resolve a dispute

1

involving a Moriori slave girl. This soon resulted in a declaration of war between the two tribes who had once been allies and friends.

Te Pahau looked across the beach to where the Ngāti Tama war party was assembling and making preparations to perform the *haka* to intimidate their enemy. This was a traditional war dance with aggressive gestures to instil fear in the enemy and lift morale in the *kaitoa*, the warriors, about to go into battle.

Choosing the beach for the showdown had been a shrewd tactical move by Te Pahau, who knew just how important footwork was in hand-to-hand combat with traditional weapons. He had carefully trained his warriors to become proficient in fighting on sand, well aware this would give them the upper hand when the time came.

Slowly, Te Pahau raised his massive *taiaha*, his preferred close-quarters combat weapon, and turned to face the men standing behind him. A long staff made from whalebone, the *taiaha* was used for stabbing thrusts and short, cutting strikes. In the hands of an experienced fighter like Te Pahau, with his almost acrobatic footwork, the *taiaha* became a devastating weapon with deadly force that had killed many an enemy on the battlefield.

'You know what to do,' said Te Pahau. 'Tūmatauenga will grant us victory if you show courage.'

With that, Te Pahau pointed his *taiaha* at the opposing war party performing the *haka* and began to jog towards them, his expression intimidating and fierce, his shrill war cry bloodcurdling.

Te Pahau was one of the first to reach the enemy. Within moments, he had dispatched two young warriors. One by slitting his throat with the sharp tip of his *taiaha*, the other by stabbing him several times in the groin.

One of the Ngāti Tama chiefs and two of his best fighters were hacking their way towards Te Pahau. This had been prearranged, as taking down Te Pahau would ensure victory and give Ngāti Tama pre-eminence on the island.

Finding Te Pahau momentarily isolated on the beach next to a fighter he had just killed, the Ngāti Tama party saw their chance. They surrounded him and began to attack him from three sides. The first attacker, a powerful young warrior, came at Te Pahau wielding a *tewhatewha,* a club with a long handle shaped like an axe. By turning on his heels, Te Pahau managed to avoid a deadly blow. At the same time, he cut his opponent's Achilles tendon from behind as he ran past him. Crying out in pain, the incapacitated attacker collapsed almost immediately, blood gushing from a large wound, turning the sand crimson.

The second attacker, also a young warrior eager to make his mark, rushed at Te Pahau with a *taiaha* just like his own, and the two engaged in a classic duel. The young warrior was no match for Te Pahau, whose superior skills soon resulted in a deep stabbing wound to his opponent's upper arm, and a deep cut to the right side of his face, severing an ear.

As Te Pahau stepped back to deliver another blow, his foot got caught on a piece of driftwood buried in the sand. Te Pahau lost his balance and fell backwards. Taking a deep breath, the injured young warrior lifted his *taiaha* and was about to thrust the sharp greenstone tip into the chest of his opponent lying in the sand, when Te Pahau rolled to one side with surprising agility, picked up his *taiaha,* and plunged it into the heart of his attacker.

What Te Pahau couldn't see while he was trying to get to his feet, was the third attacker, the Ngāti Tama chief, approaching from behind. Wielding a *mere pounamu,* a sacred weapon with spiritual qualities, which had belonged to his father and was used for close-quarter fighting, the chief sensed victory. Standing over Te Pahau, he lifted the heavy, broad-bladed greenstone club high, and then struck Te Pahau on the back of the head with all the force he could muster.

Te Pahau was dead before he collapsed into the sand. As his brain oozed through a deep crack in his skull, it mixed with the raindrops as the heavens began to weep, mourning the departure of one of the last great Māori warrior chiefs.

Pointing his weapon at Te Pahau lying in the sand, the Ngāti Tama chief let out a piercing cry of jubilation. Within moments, the fighting stopped as the combatants realised what had just happened. Effectively, the battle was over. Victory belonged to Ngāti Tama.

Nursing their wounds, the defeated Ngāti Mutunga warriors withdrew and returned to their village, leaving their dead chief behind on the battlefield.

The euphoric victors carried the body of Parema Te Pahau back to their *pā*, where his tattooed head was cut off. It would soon be turned into a treasured trophy commemorating a great victory, and serve as the centrepiece of battle stories for future generations. His corpse was then stripped naked and prepared for eating. All surviving warriors who had returned from the battlefield participated in the gruesome feast, as tradition demanded, to allow the power of their famous defeated enemy to pass to them, and give them prowess in future battles.

Palazzo da Baggio, Venice: 19 September 2023

Jack reached for the bottle in the ice bucket and looked at the countess sitting opposite. 'A little more wine?' he asked. Jack, Tristan and Countess Kuragin were having their regular Thursday night dinner in the sumptuous dining room overlooking the Grand Canal.

'Why not?' replied the countess. As she held up her glass, the maid walked in.

'A phone call for you, Contessa,' said the maid softly to the countess. 'Overseas call.'

The countess stood up, excused herself and left the room. Jack poured himself another glass of wine and turned to Tristan sitting next to him. 'Sounds important,' he said.

'It is,' replied Tristan. 'It's about me.'

'What makes you say that?' asked Jack, surprised, but was prevented from asking further questions because the countess returned, a concerned look on her face.

'It's for you, Tristan,' she said. 'Take the phone in reception.'

'What's all this about?' said Jack and handed the countess a glass of wine.

'Not sure. A call from New Zealand. I could hardly understand what the woman was saying. Funny accent. She asked for Tristan and said it was urgent.'

Looking pale, Tristan returned a few minutes later. Jack glanced at him and raised an eyebrow, the question on his face obvious. Tristan's uncanny sixth sense was well known in the family.

'It's about the Bone Scraper,' said Tristan casually.

'Now, that's a name I haven't heard in a long time,' said Jack.

'The Bone Scraper?' repeated the countess as she remembered the scary mountain of a man with the striking tattooed face, standing next to Cassandra's coffin in the chapel in Sydney thirteen years earlier. Cassandra, Tristan's mother, had been tragically killed by a hired assassin in a Broome hospital while protecting the countess's daughter, Anna, who had just been rescued in a remote cave in outback Australia.

5

'What about him?' said Jack.

'He's dying. In Auckland. Some kind of fight …'

'I see …'

'He wants to see me – urgently.'

Alarmed, the countess turned towards Tristan. 'Why?'

'He's my uncle, and my only living relative that I'm aware of.'

'That may be so,' said Jack, 'but why now? You haven't heard from him in years.'

'Apparently, he has something important to tell me. About my ancestors and destiny.'

'Ah …'

'Don't look so sceptical, Jack. I thought you of all people would understand.'

'I do,' said Jack, a little taken aback by the tone of Tristan's voice. 'I know all about destiny…'

'So, what now?' asked the countess.

'He will travel to New Zealand and talk to his uncle before he dies,' said Anna, who had just entered the room and overheard the remark.

Tristan nodded. 'Exactly.'

Tristan and Anna, a gifted painter, had a special bond. They could read each other's thoughts and communicate without talking.

'Are you sure you want to do this?' said the countess, looking worried.

'Absolutely.'

'Would you like me to come with you?' asked Jack.

'I was hoping you would say that,' replied Tristan, looking gratefully at his friend and mentor, a wry, knowing smile creasing the corners of his mouth.

'It's all settled then. I'll make the necessary arrangements and get us on the first available flight to Auckland.' Jack paused and looked around the table. 'A little more wine, anyone?'

The countess shook her head, well aware that any kind of protest about the trip would be futile.

Jack smiled as a familiar ripple of excitement made the little hairs on the back of his neck tingle. It was a familiar sensation that only occurred when another unexpected adventure came hurtling towards him out of the toolbox of destiny.

'You met the Bone Scraper at Tristan's mother's funeral, didn't you?' said Anna after Jack and Tristan had left to make travel arrangements.

'Yes, I did,' said the countess, looking apprehensive. She had never spoken about Cassandra's funeral with Anna, and Anna had stayed away from the subject, sensing it was something best left alone. Jack and Tristan had also attended the funeral, but had never spoken about it either.

Momentarily alone with her mother, Anna reached across the table and put her hand on her mother's arm. 'We've never discussed this, yet I realise that it must have been a significant event.'

'It was. Those were turbulent times and you were in hospital, recovering from an ordeal that almost killed you.'

'Then why have you never raised it with me? And neither has Tristan or Jack,' she added, a tinge of sadness in her voice.

'There were reasons.'

'You wanted to protect me?'

'You were in a bad way ...'

'But that was years ago.'

'I know. Somehow, it was never the right time.' As soon as she said it, the countess realised this sounded like a lame excuse.

'I see. As Tristan and Jack are about to travel all the way to New Zealand to talk to the Bone Scraper before he dies, could this perhaps *be* the right time?'

The countess nodded. 'I think it could be. You and Tristan are very close. You are more like brother and sister, with a special bond more than just close friends. And all of this is about Tristan's father – and destiny.'

'I thought as much. That's why I never raised it with him either. Intuition ...'

The countess turned to Anna, the touch of her daughter's hand introducing a rare moment of intimacy into the conversation between a devoted mother and a much-loved daughter, who lived in her own world and preferred to communicate through her art rather than words.

'As I said before, this is all about Tristan's father and destiny, and I suspect that's why the Bone Scraper wants to see him. And besides, Tristan is bound to tell you about all this in any case.'

Anna sat back and looked intently at her mother. 'Then it's definitely the right time, don't you think?'

The countess nodded. 'Yes, I think it is. And it's better if you hear all this from me first.'

The countess sat back and looked pensively at the da Baggio family portraits staring down on her – accusingly, she thought – from above.

'I only met the Bone Scraper once, at Cassandra's funeral in 2010. It was an unforgettable and very emotional moment, full of surprises and extraordinary revelations. This is what happened …'

Cassandra's funeral, Sydney: 13 March 2010

Cassandra's funeral was to be a quiet and private affair, with only a handful of mourners attending. Jack and Rebecca, Jack's publishing consultant, were waiting outside the church for the hearse to arrive. The countess and Professor Popov, Anna's father, sat inside in the front pew next to Andrew Simpson, the Aboriginal police officer who had played such a major part in Anna's rescue.

Tristan's sudden recovery had surprised everyone. He had insisted on coming along and was seated next to a nurse, who had accompanied him on doctor's orders. Otherwise, the church was empty.

All was quiet until the bikies turned into the street – thirty of them – riding in formation. Led by the Bone Scraper, who was wearing full Warriors regalia and sitting astride a bike with sidecar, they pulled up in front of the church, the throaty burble from their bikes all but drowning out the lonely little bell tolling in the steeple above.

'Friends of yours?' asked Rebecca, taken aback by the Warriors' unexpected appearance.

Jack didn't reply. Instead, he was remembering another funeral not that long ago, when a mother and daughter killed by terrorists had been laid to rest.

'Quiet funeral, you said?' she pressed.

The Bone Scraper and five others – all huge Māori with tattooed faces just like his – lined up on the footpath behind the hearse.

'We'll take it from here,' said the Bone Scraper to the undertakers, placing his giant hand on the coffin.

Confused, the men stepped aside. Lifting the coffin onto their broad shoulders, the Māori pallbearers walked slowly into the church.

'What are these guys doing here?' whispered Rebecca.

'Wait and see,' replied Jack.

'You knew, didn't you?' said Rebecca. Jack squeezed her hand in confirmation.

'You're a dark horse, Jack Rogan.'

'The best is yet to come – watch.'

If the celebrant waiting in front of the altar was surprised by the strange procession coming towards him, he made sure he didn't show it. Jack and Rebecca followed the coffin down the aisle and sat down next to Tristan at the front.

Jack had requested a short and simple service, and the celebrant, a friend of Will's, was about to deliver just that. Within minutes the small church was filled to capacity with unexpected mourners, as the Warriors filed in and took their seats at the back.

With the short service almost at an end, the celebrant asked if anyone wanted to say a few words. Having been told earlier there would be no eulogy, the question was merely routine.

But the Bone Scraper stood up and spoke. 'Yes, I do,' he said.

For a moment there was complete silence as all heads turned towards him. Walking slowly down the aisle until he reached the coffin, he turned and looked first at Tristan, and then at the others seated nearby.

'I owe you all an apology, and an explanation,' he began, his distinctive New Zealand accent giving his deep voice a pleasant, melodious tone.

'Firstly, I want to apologise for coming here unannounced and uninvited, but there are good reasons why that had to be so. A funeral is a solemn and serious occasion, which must be treated with respect. It is respect that brings me here. And a lot more ...'

He speaks with great eloquence, thought Jack, spellbound like all the others. A pin dropping on the stone floor would have sounded like thunder in the silent church as the Bone Scraper paused.

'Cassandra is an assumed name. Most of you would have at least suspected this, and some of you knew. But I'm sure none of you know her real name. Not even you, Tristan,' he said, looking at the frail boy sitting in the front row.

'Yet a name is very important. It tells us who we are and where we come from. Hers is a traditional name, an echo of our Māori past. She

10

and I, and my late brother, Joe, are branches of the same tree reaching back to Parema Te Pahau, a great warrior chief. Now, I'm the last one ...'

The Bone Scraper turned towards the coffin and put his hand on the lid.

'The woman lying in this box is my sister, Ina Te Papatahi,' he said quietly. 'That's why I'm here.' Staring at the coffin, the Bone Scraper paused again, not sure if he should go on. 'She had a twin,' he said at last. 'Our brother, Joe. She and Joe were one. Now they are together again.'

The Bone Scraper stood in silence for what seemed an eternity, his striking face like chiselled stone. Then softly, he began to chant in Māori. He was saying goodbye to a younger sister he had lost along the way, only to find her again when it was already too late. After a while, the chanting turned to a whisper, and then stopped completely. Turning around, the Bone Scraper looked straight ahead and stared at something only he could see, before walking slowly back to his pew and beginning to sing.

As the haunting Māori farewell to the dead rose to the rafters, the Warriors stood as one and joined in. What had started as a quiet service had turned into an unexpected celebration of an amazing life.

At the conclusion of the funeral, the Māori pallbearers stepped forward again and carried the coffin outside. The Bone Scraper placed it carefully on the waiting sidecar, dismissed the funeral director, and sent the hearse away. In line with club tradition, Cassandra – Ina Te Papatahi – would be taken to the cemetery in style, and then laid to rest next to her twin brother, Joe.

* * *

Mesmerised, Anna listened in silence without interrupting and waited until her mother had finished.

'So, now we know who Tristan's mother really was,' said Anna.

'Cassandra was a Māori princess by the name of Ina Te Papatahi, and she had two brothers. A twin brother, Joe, and the Bone Scraper.'

'But you said that this was all about Tristan's *father*, and destiny, yet you haven't mentioned his father once. Why's that?'

The countess again turned to Anna and began to stroke her hair. 'I haven't spoken about Tristan's father because it's too painful,' she said, her voice quavering with emotion. 'And also profoundly disturbing,' she added softly.

Anna nodded. 'Did the Bone Scraper talk about him at the funeral?'

'No. But Jack spoke with him later, when he did some research for the book he was writing at the time—'

'About me and my disappearance in the Outback?'

'Yes. That's when the Bone Scraper talked about Tristan's father.'

'Jack knows all about this, then?'

'Yes, he does, and so does Tristan. Most of it, I think.'

'Yet they never spoke to me about any of this? Why's that, do you think?'

Searching for the right words so as not to hurt Anna, the countess hesitated before answering. 'Tristan didn't want you to know who his real father was.'

'Oh? *Why?*'

'I think it's better if you hear this from him. I'm sure he will tell you when the time's right,' replied the countess, close to tears.

'Very well.' Anna stood up and walked to the door. As she reached the door she stopped and turned around. 'I had no idea we had so many secrets,' she said, the sadness in her voice obvious.

'All families have secrets. When Tristan tells you about his father, you will understand.'

'I hope so. Goodnight, Mama,' said Anna and left the room.

On the way to Auckland: 21 September 2023

'It's good to have friends in the travel business,' said Jack, stretching out in his comfortable Business Class seat as the plane began to climb to its cruising altitude after leaving Venice. 'These two airline tickets are worth their weight in gold.'

'Sure,' said Tristan, seated next to Jack. 'We have to change planes in Singapore?'

'Yes. We should be there in about thirteen hours.'

'And from there to Auckland?'

'Another ten. We are going halfway around the world, remember?'

'Enough time, then …'

'Time for what?'

'To tell me what you found out about my family all those years ago.'

'What do you mean?'

'You know exactly what I mean. Let's go back to that fateful evening after my mother's funeral in March 2010.'

'Ah. That evening in June at the Kuragin chateau. You were living with the countess in France by then. Going to school in a French village close by, right? And speaking reasonable French already. Must have been quite an adjustment.'

Tristan looked at Jack with sad eyes. 'It was, but love makes everything possible. I had become a member of her family. She took me in after my mother died and treated me like a son. Still does. And you had just arrived from the airport.'

'And you from school on your bicycle, if I remember correctly. We hadn't seen each other since the funeral in Sydney.'

'That's right. And you had brought your manuscript with you and were going to show it to us: *The Disappearance of Anna Popov.*'

'I remember.'

'Then you will also remember what happened later that evening,' said Tristan.

'I do. You had gone to bed, Anna was in her studio, and her parents, the countess and Professor Popov, and I—'

'Were discussing the extraordinary things you had found out about my family. You were all in the dining room.'

'That's right.'

'And, of course, you remember what happened next?'

'How could I forget? Suddenly, there you were. A little boy in pyjamas standing next to the piano in the adjacent room, *listening*. We were all stunned, and concerned—'

'Because I may have overheard some disturbing revelations you had discovered about my father?'

'Yes. Disturbing would be an understatement.'

'Except that I had already known all about that. Well, most of it anyway.'

'Yes, you surprised us all when you told us. We were quite shocked.'

'Have you ever wondered how much of what you were talking about I *had* actually overheard?'

'Yes, of course; still do.'

'But you never spoke about it. You never asked me. Why was that?'

'We thought it was better that way. For you, I mean. Just in case. Remember, you were thirteen at the time. Young, vulnerable. Some things in life are best left alone.'

'I don't agree. Look at me now. I'm twenty-six, and we are on our way to New Zealand to talk with my uncle on his deathbed, because he wants to tell me something about my ancestors and destiny. Don't you think I should know what you had found out about my family *before* we talk to him?'

Jack turned towards Tristan and looked at him pensively; the argument was persuasive. 'I think you're right,' he said, the storyteller in him trying to find the right way to approach this sensitive subject. 'Where to begin?' Jack mused.

'The beginning is always a good place to start, don't you think? If you really want to know, I overheard very little of what you were talking about that night, except for who my father was. But then, I already knew all about that.'

'Yes, you said.'

'But there was a lot more, wasn't there?'

'Yes, there was.'

'All right then. Here we are, you and me, thirty-thousand feet above ground, racing through the night in a machine, strapped into comfortable seats with nowhere to go. The perfect place for a heart-to-heart, don't you think?' said Tristan, trying to make Jack, who was clearly quite tense, feel more at ease.

'I suppose so. Let's have a drink and I'll tell you.'

'Good idea. Brandy?'

'Perfect.'

'Well, I think the best way to tell you what I found out is to tell you a story,' said Jack, sipping his cognac. 'After all, that's what I do best.'

'True.'

'It all began in a travelling circus in Australia, owned by the parents of a young man called Eugene, thirty or so years ago. Eugene was the strong man, and his Māori friend, nicknamed the Bone Scraper, was his sidekick. They were part of an acrobatic act, the Flying Kiwis, would you believe?

'The youngest and most exciting members of the troupe were the Bone Scraper's siblings: a teenager called Cassandra and her twin brother, Joe. In a way, it was a family affair. They were the star attraction.

'Cassandra could contort her body in ways that seemed impossible, and both of them could do somersaults that had the audience gasping. Then one day, Cassandra had a terrible accident. Joe missed his timing. His hands just weren't there when his sister came flying through the air. Cassandra broke a hip and a leg. Badly. The doctors thought she would never walk again. But in a circus, everyone has to pull their weight. The boys found a new girl and Cassandra, by now a cripple, became a fortune teller.'

'So, that's how it all began,' said Tristan. 'I had been wondering about that.'

'Yes, and that one tragic incident set an astonishing chain of events in train, with consequences years later that are difficult to imagine.' Jack held up his empty glass, a signal for the flight attendant to refill it.

'Eugene's mother, a colourful gypsy who dabbled in the occult,' continued Jack, 'introduced Cassandra to the tarot. Soon after that, Eugene got into trouble with the law and went to jail. The Bone Scraper followed in his footsteps and the Flying Kiwis were no more. For several years, Joe stayed with the circus and looked after Cassandra, until one day, Eugene returned. Fresh out of jail and with nowhere to go, he wanted to join the circus again. By now, Cassandra, the girl, had grown into an attractive young woman, with a boyfriend – a talented young juggler from Argentina called Merlin – the new star attraction. The scene was set for trouble. Big trouble—'

'This was all in your manuscript, the book you didn't publish?'

'Yes, it was all in *The Disappearance of Anna Popov*, which, much to the frustration and dismay of my publisher, was never released.'

'Why did you decide to do that?' asked Tristan. 'I've often wondered about that.'

'Yet you never asked.'

'No. I knew it had to be something very personal and private. And because of that, you would tell me one day, or not.'

'Very perceptive of you, as usual. Well, it looks like the day has arrived.'

'Seems that way. Is it because we are going to see the Bone Scraper?'

'Yes, I suppose it is. He is the last person alive who played a central part in this story. The last actor to take a bow before the final curtain call.'

'Sounds dramatic.'

'It is. This story has it all, in more ways than you can possibly imagine. When I wrote it all down, I thought it sounded more like Shakespearian fiction than fact, and that my readers would see it the same way. But that's all academic now.'

'Any regrets?'

'About not having published the book?'

'Aha.'

'None at all. It was the right decision at the time, and it still is.'

Jack paused and ran his fingers through his hair. This helped him collect his thoughts when tackling a difficult subject.

'A writer has a responsibility,' he continued. 'What I discovered during my research – especially my conversations with the Bone Scraper – was a remarkable story of tragedy and love, of deep suffering and acts of selfless sacrifice, but at the same time, it was a story that had a dark side as well. A very dark one that had the power to ruin lives, affect generations, and send ripples of pain and discord well into the future.'

'Wow! Powerful words. Especially coming from you,' said Tristan.

'Suppose so. Over the years, I thought very long and hard about how to tell you all this one day. I think the best way to prepare the way, is to tell you a little about myself first.'

'Good idea. More often than not you're a dark horse, Jack. Difficult to read.'

'Is that so? Even to someone like you?' teased Jack.

'Yes.'

'There's really no mystery about all this. Writing a book is a lonely business. It gives you plenty of time to think and reflect. I wrote most of this one alone, in Will's house, surrounded by all the memories that place held for me. As you know, he was my closest friend, and his family was my family. A bit like the Kuragin family has become yours.'

Tristan reached for Jack's hand and squeezed it in a gesture of deep friendship and affection. Jack squeezed Tristan's hand in silent reply, and then continued.

'It would be an understatement to say that Anna's story is as extraordinary as it is unique. It is unique because it isn't fiction. It's based on real events and deals with the lives of real people. This alone would have guaranteed the success of the book. When we add to this the unprecedented publicity and media interest surrounding Anna's return, the sky would have been the limit. But at what cost?' Jack paused and looked at Tristan.

'Often, life throws you in at the deep end and it's up to you, and you alone, to reach the safety of the shore,' said Jack. 'Some succeed, others don't. I believe I just made it to the shore on that occasion. It wasn't easy; I almost drowned.'

'Apart from all else, this is quite a story,' said Tristan, realising just how personal these matters were to Jack.

'It was all part of my journey of becoming a writer. Fortunately, I listened to the little voices in my head—'

'The whisper of angels?' ventured Tristan, smiling.

'Who knows? Call it conscience, knowing right from wrong, whatever. That's why I decided not to publish and expose the book to a sensation-hungry world, to be picked over until only the bare bones were left for all to see. I couldn't live with that.'

'I understand,' said Tristan, 'but I obviously need to know more. There is more, isn't there?'

'There sure is. More than you can possibly imagine. I just hope you're ready for this.'

'Come on, Jack. How much longer were you going to wait and keep this from me? Once I speak with the Bone Scraper – if he's still alive by the time we get to see him – he's bound to talk about all these things. Just think how it would look if I were to hear all this for the first time. From a dying man!'

'You're right, mate. I just need a little quiet time to collect my thoughts before we continue. There's plenty of time. We aren't going anywhere. I think I'll have a little nap.'

'You can be so exasperating at times!' said Tristan. 'This isn't a page-turner in one of your novels, to keep your readers on their toes. This is real life we're talking about here.'

'I know,' said Jack and closed his eyes.

Stopover in Singapore: 22 September

The connecting flight to Auckland was delayed by five hours. This gave Jack and Tristan ample time to explore one of the most exciting attractions of the Singapore Airport precinct: Jewel Changi.

Opened in October 2019, Jewel Changi – a unique, nature-themed entertainment and retail complex – had it all. Its breathtaking features included the Rain Vortex, the world's tallest indoor waterfall; the Shiseido Forest Valley, a magnificent, five-storey indoor garden with three thousand trees and sixty thousand shrubs at the bottom; and the Canopy Park at the top, which featured the Topiary Walk and the Petal Garden. With three hundred thousand visitors per day, Jewel Changi was one of the most visited tourist attractions in the world.

Jack had chosen the stunning centrepiece of the complex – the Canopy Bridge, a suspension bridge twenty-three metres above ground level, with a panoramic view of the Rain Vortex – as the place to tell Tristan the painful truth about his father.

'Wow! This is really something,' said Tristan, watching the waterfall cascade from an enormous round opening in the glass roof forty metres above ground level, into a sparkling pool at the bottom.

'Recirculating rainwater, thirty-seven thousand litres of it, pumped from the pool down there to the rooftop up here every minute; an engineering marvel. Ingenious, and unique.' Jack paused, collecting his thoughts.

'The way the Wizard, your father, died was ingenious – and unique too, in a bizarre kind of way – and it was all the Bone Scraper's idea. *Ars Moriendi*,' continued Jack.

'What do you mean?' asked Tristan, frowning.

'For you to understand what happened to your father, I have to tell you about my first meeting with the Bone Scraper.' For a while, Jack watched the waterfall, and then turned to face Tristan. 'This is what happened,' he said, placing a hand on Tristan's right shoulder.

Warriors' clubhouse: 8 March 2010, 10 pm

Jack knew he was late. He switched off the bike and looked around. The derelict panel-beating shop appeared deserted in the dark. Most of the windows were broken and the doors were boarded up. Two rusty car bodies without wheels were blocking the driveway, their headlights staring at Jack like eyes of guard dogs watching. Jack was about to check the address again to make sure he was in the right place when he heard sounds coming from somewhere out the back – the clinking of iron against iron, and a slapping sound. *Weights and punching bags,* thought Jack, dismounting. *A gym.*

As he walked past the car bodies, Jack saw something move. A dark shape materialised from the shadows in front of him.

'Looking for something, mate?' it asked, coming closer.

'Yes – the Bone Scraper,' replied Jack.

'Wait here.'

Suddenly, floodlights came on above him, illuminating a large yard. Momentarily blinded, Jack closed his eyes. When he opened them again, he was looking at two huge men, both Māori, standing directly in front of him.

'Turn around and hold up your hands where I can see them,' said one of the hulks. Jack felt a pair of hands running down his back and legs.

'Clean,' said the man behind him. 'Come with me.'

Jack followed the man across the yard, past rows of gleaming bikes, to an open steel door. Inside, he could see several men lifting weights so heavy, they made the steel rods bend. The two fans turning lazily overhead did little to stir the stale air, heavy with the acrid smell of sweat and diesel.

'That's him over there,' said the man, pointing to a wrestling mat in the middle of the room. 'The one on top.'

Wearing only loincloths, the two men on the mat reminded Jack of sumo wrestlers, only taller and more muscular. Each had his long black hair pulled back and tied into a knot. The man on top had his opponent pinned to the mat.

'Concede,' he barked.

Barely able to breathe, the man lying face down on the mat nodded. The bout was over. The winner disengaged, rolled away with surprising agility, and stood up. Towering over Jack, he picked up a towel and looked at him. His massive arms, buttocks and back were heavily tattooed with Māori motifs, but most striking of all was his *moko*. In the old days, the *moko* – the traditional Māori facial decoration – was applied with a chisel that left grooves in the skin. In more recent times, the tattoo needle had replaced the chisel, leaving the skin smooth. Delicate scrolls, dots and fine lines – especially around the mouth and forehead – accentuated the prominent features of the Bone Scraper's face, making him look like a carving of a Māori god come to life.

'A bout like this is better than the *haka*,' he said, wiping his face. 'The *haka* only intimidates; this ends in victory or defeat. That's why I like to wrestle – it prepares you for the real thing. You're the journalist whose house burned down?'

Jack nodded. He hadn't mentioned anything about this on the phone.

'I know how it feels.'

'Cassandra's dead,' said Jack.

'I heard. Why are you here?'

'I made her a promise. On her deathbed.'

'Tell me about it.'

Jack followed the Bone Scraper around the gym and explained why he had come and what he had in mind. Listening carefully, the Bone Scraper was evaluating Jack's proposal. He was used to making quick decisions and taking risks. If there was a chance – however remote – of getting even with his old foe, the Wizard, he was in. The only real question was the commitment of the man standing in front of him, and the accuracy of the intelligence he was providing. Without that, this couldn't work.

The Bone Scraper's own sources had already confirmed most of what Jack was telling him, but there was something new that could change everything: *a tunnel*. The Wolf's Lair compound was built like a fortress, with sophisticated, round-the-clock electronic surveillance and security systems covering every square centimetre. It was impossible to enter the place undetected, unless Cassandra was right about the tunnel. But what really tipped the scales in favour of the daring plan was the fact the man telling him all this was taking most of the risk and had a hell of a lot to lose. This was the kind of insurance the Bone Scraper liked.

'Do you understand what you're proposing?' he asked, watching Jack carefully. 'This is war. Once you start, there's no turning back, for us or you.'

Jack nodded.

'It's like breaking my opponent's neck here on the mat a moment ago, rather than letting him go. Are you prepared for that?'

'Yes.'

'When's all this supposed to happen?'

'Tonight. After I leave here, I'm going to see the Wizard. He's kind of expecting me. The police will raid the compound in a few hours. I'll know exactly when. That gives you a small window—'

'Something puzzles me,' interrupted the Bone Scraper.

'What?'

'Why isn't the Wizard leaving with the others? What makes you so sure he'll be there, virtually alone? Waiting for the police, and for you?'

'That's been troubling me, too. You know the Wizard better than most. I believe the answer is right there in his character: pride, bravado, arrogance. He likes to taunt and show off. He believes he can beat the system, and to do that, he mustn't violate his bail conditions. He has to remain at the compound and report to the police daily. He can't abscond – *pride* won't let him. And besides, the police will find nothing incriminating. He's already made sure of that. *Bravado*. That's why the compound's been evacuated. As usual, his police contacts have tipped him off, giving him plenty of time to cover his tracks. It's the same with this tunnel.'

'What do you mean?'

'His obsession with security is both a strength and a weakness. The whole place is protected like Fort Knox. But he has to have a secret escape route only he and a couple of his close cronies know about. That's why there are no alarms, no surveillance, nothing. *Arrogance*. He kept it all to himself.'

Impressed, the Bone Scraper nodded. 'And the boy – Tristan?' he asked. 'If you're right, he won't be there. Not with the police coming.'

'No, but the Wizard will know where he is.'

'The boy may be dead.'

'I don't think so.'

'How come?'

'The moment Cassandra died, her son became worthless. Why kill him? Why take the risk? Especially now, with the spotlight of the law on the Wizards. No, the boy's alive and I'm going to find him,' said Jack.

'But you don't need me for that, do you? You have your own ways ...'

This was the one question Jack had been dreading. It was the one flaw in his argument and it hadn't taken the Bone Scraper long to find it. It was time to come clean.

'Strictly speaking, no. But there were two parts to my promise.'

'Oh?'

'Cassandra's son, and ...'

'And?'

'*Retribution*. Cassandra said that you of all people would understand – and act.'

The Bone Scraper traced one of the tattoos on his chin with an index finger. The finger went round and round, following the intricate scrolls engraved onto his skin. He always did this when he was about to make an important decision. Then, the finger stopped.

'You don't know, do you?' he said after a while. 'About Tiki Joe?'

'What about him?'

'You don't know who he was, do you?'

'I don't understand,' said Jack, looking puzzled.

'You'll find out. Another time.'

'Are you in, Parema Te Pahau?' Cassandra had briefed Jack well.

The Bone Scraper looked up, surprised. Just like the Wizard, he was very superstitious. How come this *Pākehā* knew his true name? he wondered. Was it a sign?

'The Bone Scraper claims to be a direct descendant of Parema Te Pahau, a famous Māori warrior chief who lived in the 1800s and was one of the last cannibals. He was known as the Bone Scraper,' Jack said.

'I'm in,' he said.

'If the Wizard lives, we're both dead,' said Jack, holding out his hand.

Finally convinced that Jack understood what he was in for, the Bone Scraper relaxed a little.

'You well before me, my friend,' he said and shook Jack's hand. 'Now, tell me more about this tunnel.'

Auckland: 23 September 2023

It was almost dark by the time the plane landed in Auckland.

'Well, we made it,' said Jack, rubbing his stiff neck after the long flight from Singapore. 'Seems like we've been flying forever.'

'Feels that way,' said Tristan, his face flushed with excitement. 'I can't wait!'

'Wait?' What for?'

'To meet the Bone Scraper.'

'Ah. You can obviously sense something,' ventured Jack.

'Sure can.'

'What might that be?'

'Destiny,' said Tristan.

'I suspected something like that.'

'Could be scary.'

'Trying to frighten me?' said Jack.

'Hardly. You've met the guy before; I haven't. I've only seen him once – at my mother's funeral. But from what you've told me about him in Singapore …'

Jack waved dismissively. 'Let's see … You said someone was going to meet us at the airport?'

'That's what I was told.'

Jack got out of his seat and stood up. 'We'll find out soon enough, I suppose,' he said and reached for his hand luggage.

Jack was the first to notice the two Māori standing at the back of the crowded hall. Towering over everyone else – with tattooed faces and their long hair tied into a knot at the back of the head, giving them a threatening appearance – they looked conspicuous in the busy International Arrivals Hall.

People were giving them a wide berth, and two security guards standing behind them were keeping a close eye on the unwelcome intruders, to make sure there was no trouble.

The only thing that didn't fit was the cardboard sign held up by one of the men, with 'TRISTAN' written across in large letters. Both men looked uncomfortable and out of place in their leather vests and gang colours, radiating danger.

'Our welcoming committee, I'd say,' said Jack and pointed to the Māori with the sign. 'Come, let's say hello.'

'As long as we don't have to rub noses with them, we should be fine,' said Tristan, referring to the *hongi*, the traditional Māori greeting.

'Let's find out. They've come to meet you, not me,' teased Jack as he began to make his way over to the waiting men.

'You Tristan?' growled one of the men as Jack approached.

'No. He is. I'm Jack.'

'What took you so long? We've been waiting hours. We must hurry. He's in a bad way.'

'Who is?' asked Tristan.

'The Bone Scraper. Car's just outside. Let's go!'

The crowd parted as the two Māori made their way to the exit. Jack and Tristan followed dutifully behind. The car, parked illegally directly in front of the exit, reminded Jack of Cuba. A huge, battered 1959 Chevrolet Impala with Māori motifs painted all over its bonnet – an eyebrow-raising curiosity that had attracted the attention of the traffic wardens – was about to be towed away. A tow truck was backing slowly towards the car. One of the Māori walked over to the truck and began to shout at the driver through the open window. 'What do you think you're doing, bro?'

Ignoring the question, the driver got out of the truck and began to attach a chain to the Chevrolet's bumper bar. 'What does it look like?' he said. 'This piece of shit is blocking the entire drop-off area.'

The Māori yanked the chain out of the tow truck driver's hands, sending him staggering backwards, and glared at him. 'We're just leaving; piss off!'

A policeman, who had been watching the altercation, walked up to the Māori. 'What's going on?' he asked, sensing trouble.

'Nothing we can't handle, officer. This moron was about to damage my car. I just stopped him in time, that's all. We are leaving, in any case.'

'Good idea,' said the officer, relieved, and turned to Jack. 'You are with them?' he asked, lowering his voice.

'We are. We've just arrived.'

'Do you know who these guys are?'

'Not really. They've come to meet us ...'

'They belong to the Black Arrows. One of the most dangerous gangs in New Zealand,' said the officer, giving Jack a stern look.

Jack shrugged.

'Suit yourself. I hope you know what you're doing. These guys live in a different world. Be careful.'

'Will do, officer. Thanks,' said Jack cheerfully.

'You coming, or what?' said one of the Māori, holding the car boot open. Jack walked over to him and put his duffel bag into the boot, next to an assortment of iron bars and baseball bats, tried and tested implements of frequent gangland wars raging in Auckland. As soon as Jack and Tristan got into the back seat, the powerful V8 engine roared into life.

'Cocky bastard,' said the Māori driving the car, and pulled away from the kerb, missing the stunned tow truck driver by inches.

Black Arrows' clubhouse, Auckland: 23 September

The trip from the airport to the southern outskirts of Auckland turned into a white-knuckle ride difficult to forget. How the cumbersome vintage car managed to take corners at such breakneck speed – tyres screeching – without hitting the kerb was a mystery. Jack resisted the urge to ask the Māori driver, who seemed to be enjoying himself, to slow down. Conversation with Tristan was impossible due to the blaring reggae music, the deafening base making the seats shake.

The Black Arrows are one of the most dangerous gangs in New Zealand; be careful', Jack heard the policeman say. *Too late*, he thought and closed his eyes. He opened them again when he could feel the car slow down as it entered a dilapidated industrial area littered with abandoned car bodies and broken furniture. The stray dogs rummaging through rubbish added to the desperation of the district.

'Here we are,' said the Māori in the passenger seat as the car pulled up in front of what looked like a large corrugated-iron shed, a solid steel gate with razor wire on top blocking the entrance.

The driver honked the horn. Moments later, a small peephole-like opening in the steel door opened. Obviously, someone was having a look.

The driver waved and slowly, the massive gate opened.

Jack turned to Tristan sitting next to him. 'It's another world, all right,' he said as the car drove into an enclosed courtyard and came to a sudden halt in front of what looked like open, flood-lit workshops with cars on hoists being repaired by sweaty, bare-chested mechanics. There was also a gym with a dozen or so Māori youths working out.

The scene reminded Jack of his visit to the clubhouse of the Warriors, an outlaw motorcycle gang in Sydney, where he had met the Bone Scraper for the first time.

'Satan's panel-beating shop for lost souls? What do you think?' said Tristan and opened the door.

'Welcome to hell, you mean? Hieronymus Bosch would have loved this,' said Jack.

'Inspiration for one of his paintings, do you think?'

'Aha. Certainly reminds me of his work. Your relatives, mate, not mine,' replied Jack and got out of the car.

The driver walked over to a tall, grey-haired Māori watching them, and pointed to Tristan. Jack thought he looked vaguely familiar. The grey-haired Māori nodded and approached Tristan. 'Just in time,' he said. 'Follow me.'

Tristan pointed to Jack standing next to him. 'This is Jack, a friend. He has met the Bone Scraper before.'

'I remember. He got shot by the Undertaker the night the Wizard died.'

Of course, thought Jack as he remembered that fateful night at the Wolf's Lair. Jack touched the scar on his forehead, a reminder of a deadly bullet that narrowly missed his brain.

'Wait here,' growled the Māori and went inside. He returned moments later. 'All right. You can both come in, but first I have to pat you down; house rules. Spread your legs and raise your hands ...'

Satisfied, the Māori turned around. 'Follow me, but I have to warn you, he's in a bad way.'

Jack looked at Tristan, raised an eyebrow and pointed to an open, rusty door. 'After you, mate. Prepare yourself.'

As soon as Jack entered what looked like a workshop smelling of paint and diesel, he stopped and looked around to allow his eyes to become accustomed to the gloom.

A space had been cleared in the middle of the otherwise cluttered, windowless chamber, which had previously been used for spray-painting. The only light intruding hesitantly into the darkness came from a single light globe dangling from the corrugated-iron ceiling. It cast a pale circle of light on the grimy concrete floor, illuminating it like a stage in some bizarre play with only one actor.

The Bone Scraper sat in a high-backed lounge chair, its horsehair-stuffed armrests torn around the edges. Bare-chested, with bandages crisscrossing his massive, hairy torso, he locked eyes with Tristan, staring at him.

'Come closer, where I can see you,' said the Bone Scraper, his deep, resonant voice sounding otherworldly, like the voice of some Greek oracle revealing secrets of the future.

Both Tristan and Jack took a few steps forward.

'Ah, Jack. Good of you to come as well. We meet again. Times have changed. Look at me now.'

'What happened?' asked Jack.

The Bone Scraper lifted his hand slowly and pointed to his bandaged chest. 'A fight. What else? Knives. After all, we once were warriors,' he said with sadness in his voice.

Jack watched the Bone Scraper sitting as if strapped into what looked like some weird ejector seat into the afterlife, and wondered ...

'You were there when the Wizard was dying. *Ars Moriendi*, remember?' continued the Bone Scraper with a wry smile. 'We gave him quite a send-off, didn't we?'

'You sure did. I would call it unforgettable. Retribution would be more accurate, just as Cassandra had predicted.'

'He had to pay the ferryman before he was allowed to cross to the other side.'

'Some payment,' said Jack, remembering that fateful night at the Wolf's Lair.

'Now, it's my turn,' said the Bone Scraper. 'If I had listened to the medicos, I would be lying somewhere in a hospital bed with tubes hanging out of my chest. That was never going to be for me. This place may not look it, but it's infinitely better than that. It's part of my world.'

Exhausted, the Bone Scraper paused and looked at Tristan. 'Tristan, it's time,' he said.

'Time for what?' asked Tristan.

'You *know* what. You are the last one. It's your turn now. Death is just another path. Nothing to be afraid of. It's how we deal with it is all that matters. There isn't much time, and I have a lot to tell you. Come, have a good look at my face, because very soon that will be the lasting memory of me, and I want you to take it with you,' said the Bone Scraper. He was beginning to choke and blood had begun trickling from the corners of his mouth.

'You have to complete what I've begun. You have to succeed where I have failed. You are our only hope ...' continued the Bone Scraper, his voice barely audible.

Tristan walked into the circle of light and stood facing the Bone Scraper.

'Jack, please leave us. This is between Tristan, our ancestors, and me,' whispered the Bone Scraper.

Jack nodded and walked towards the door.

'It's all about destiny,' added the Bone Scraper just before Jack reached the door. 'We can't escape destiny. I'm sure you understand that better than most.'

'I do,' said Jack and left the room.

Tristan came out of the chamber half an hour later, his ashen face drawn. Jack had never seen him like that before. He looked as if he had seen something terrifying, like a ghost from a violent past. The grey-haired Māori walked up to Tristan standing at the open door.

'Has he gone?' he asked.

Tristan nodded. As the Māori raised his hand, the entire complex fell silent and men came from all sides and stood in front of the open door. Five men, all elderly Māori, their heavily tattooed faces looking grim, stepped forward and followed the grey-haired man inside. Moments later, chanting could be heard as the men came out of the room, carrying the dead Bone Scraper on their broad shoulders, as tradition demanded.

'Me tangi, kāpā ko te mate i te marama.'

Soon, all the others joined in. It reminded Jack of Cassandra's funeral, where the same eerie, moving song had filled the chapel as her coffin had been carried outside on similar shoulders.

As the strange procession passed Tristan, it stopped momentarily. 'You, come with us,' said one of the Māori elders carrying the Bone Scraper's limp body. Tristan nodded and fell in behind them.

Jack was about to do the same when someone placed a big hand on his shoulder from behind. 'Not you,' said a deep voice.

Jack nodded and stood respectfully to attention as the body was carried past him.

Jack was invited to sit with a group of Māori, singing and drinking beer, in what seemed like an improvised wake. All work in the complex had stopped, out of respect for the departed.

When Tristan returned an hour or so later, surrounded by a group of elders, Jack gasped. A striking Māori tattoo, a traditional *moko* covering the right side of his face, had transformed Tristan's appearance. His handsome features had turned into a tribal reminder of a violent past, a link to a famous ancestor whose revered memory lived on and was being celebrated by all those present.

'We are staying as guests in one of the Māori homes tonight before we get on the ship,' said Tristan, sitting next to Jack in the back of the vintage club car.

'On the *ship*?' asked Jack. 'We are going somewhere?'

'We are.'

'Where?'

'Chatham Islands.'

Jack nodded but decided not to pursue the matter further. 'Care to tell me what happened while you were with the Bone Scraper?' he asked instead, changing direction.

'Later,' said Tristan, waving dismissively. He was tracing the outline of his new facial tattoo with his fingertips. 'This is only the first outline. There will be follow-up procedures. Tradition.'

'All right,' said Jack, realising Tristan had to be left alone with his thoughts. Jack was holding on as the car screeched around corners at breakneck speed.

By the time they arrived at the modest home in a poor, working-class neighbourhood, a rowdy party was already in full swing. Loud music boomed through the open front door, and crates of beer almost blocked the crowded hallway. Tristan and his new *moko* were a curiosity. Giggling girls and burly, heavily tattooed youths kept pointing to his face, their manner jovial, but respectful.

After several hours of heavy drinking, the guests left and the music became softer. An elderly Māori woman who obviously lived in the house showed Tristan and Jack to a room at the back. 'Ship leaves at sunrise. I'll wake you and cook breakfast,' she said, smiling, and left the room.

Tristan lay down on one of the narrow beds and closed his eyes.

'Quite a day, mate,' said Jack. 'Is this what you expected?'

'No. This was more than I could have imagined.'

Jack sat down on the other narrow bed in the room but didn't reply. He knew Tristan would tell him more when he was ready.

'You know all about promises, Jack, don't you?' began Tristan after a while, his voice hoarse.

'I do.'

'I made a promise today and gave my word to a dying man; my uncle,' said Tristan.

'What kind of promise?'

Tristan opened his eyes, sat up, and looked at Jack. 'To find the head of one of my ancestors and bring it back here for burial.'

'That's quite a promise,' said Jack, raising an eyebrow. 'Can you tell me more?'

'We are talking about Parema Te Pahau. A famous Māori chief and warrior. The Bone Scraper is named after him. Parema Te Pahau is his real name.'

'I know.'

'Then you would also know that the Bone Scraper's facial tattoo was inspired by the *moko* on the famous chief's face.'

'The Bone Scraper told me. And this is relevant because...?'

'I now wear part of that very tattoo on my face, right here.' Tristan pointed to his right cheek. 'It's an exact copy of the Bone Scraper's tattoo. This should help, but it may not be enough,' said Tristan.

'You speak in riddles. Please elaborate.'

'This is quite a tale. Taking a leaf out of your book, I'll tell you a story.'

'Always the best way,' replied Jack, smiling. 'I'm a good listener.'

'It all began during the bloody Musket Wars in 1825. You have heard of them, surely?' said Tristan.

'Sure have. The European settlers brought muskets to New Zealand, and the warlike native tribes soon discovered their devastating effect in battle and began to acquire them through trade. This resulted in an arms race between tribes who all wanted to gain the upper hand.'

'Very good. How come you know all this?'

'Research. I looked into Māori history and customs when I wrote *The Disappearance of Anna Popov*. And besides, I interviewed the Bone Scraper on several occasions, and he spoke a lot about these wars, and Māori history and tradition. Apparently, more than twenty thousand Māori died in battle during these wars, which began in about 1820, lasted around two decades, and wiped out almost twenty per cent of the entire Māori population.'

'Dreadful as that must have been, this sets the scene for the story I'm about to tell you, because the event that had such a far-reaching impact on my family took place in 1835 on the Chatham Islands.'

'Fascinating,' said Jack.

'Parema Te Pahau was a revered chief of Ngāti Mutunga, an *iwi*, or tribe, living in the Wellington region. But they felt unsafe and threatened by neighbouring tribes, always on the lookout for more land and conquests. Weakened by frequent inter-tribal wars, a decision was made in 1835 by tribal elders to leave Ngāti Mutunga land and migrate to the Chatham Islands. They gifted their land to neighbouring tribes, burned the bones of their ancestors, and left.'

'That's quite a decision to make.'

'Sure was. Apparently, Chief Parema Te Pahau had a lot to do with this because he was a *tohunga matakite*, a foreteller of the future. There were about eight hundred Ngāti Mutunga ready to leave their home, and how they made it to the Chatham Islands is a story worthy of a movie. Ingenious, and bold.'

'Oh? Tell me.'

'In November 1835, Mutunga warriors hijacked the brig *Lord Rodney* in Port Nicholson, today's Wellington, and forced the crew to sail to the Chatham Islands. With several hundred souls and a vast amount of supplies and livestock on board, the ship left Port Nicholson and sailed to the Chatham Islands, where the newcomers were welcomed by the peace-loving Moriori population. This had catastrophic consequences for the local Moriori, who were slaughtered by the invaders and not only took their land, but also enslaved the survivors.'

'Brutal times,' said Jack, shaking his head.

'Perhaps, seen through the lens of history, but to the invading tribes this was nothing unusual, because taking possession of the land in that way was entirely in accord with custom.'

'Interesting.'

'All seemed to be working well between the invading tribes until 1840, when the Ngāti Mutunga decided to attack Ngāti Tama, their former allies. A bloody battle ensued, during which many were killed. Parema Te Pahau was one of them, and that's when it all began.'

'What exactly?'

'Killing the chief of their opponent in battle was seen as a major victory by Ngāti Tama. The jubilant victors paraded his body through their *pā* – their village – before cutting off his heavily tattooed head, and then eating the rest of the corpse.'

'That's quite a victory celebration to digest. And to think that this wasn't that long ago. Local custom, I suppose,' said Jack.

'It was. Eating your enemy was the ultimate victory, and annihilation of their power and spirit. The Māori believed that as the defeated enemy's flesh passed through the body, there was a transfer of power to the victor. As Parema Te Pahau was well known not only for his prowess on the battlefield, but also for his spiritual powers, this was viewed as a significant event.'

'Obviously that didn't include his head, because you made a promise.'

'To find it and bring it back for burial, because until that happens, the soul cannot pass into the afterlife and take its rightful place next to the ancestors.'

'Any idea what happened to it?' asked Jack.

Tristan shook his head and closed his eyes. 'By then, the Bone Scraper was almost incoherent and could barely speak, but he did give me a significant clue just before he died.'

'What kind of clue?'

'He said I should go and talk to someone who may be able to help. Someone who lives on the Chatham Islands.'

'*Who?*'

Tristan turned to face the wall for what seemed a long time and didn't reply. Jack thought he must have fallen asleep.

'My grandmother,' whispered Tristan softly after a while, with pain and sadness in his voice as he remembered the Bone Scraper's death and his own mother's funeral, before drifting into a restless slumber.

On the way to the Chatham Islands: 24 September

Jack and Tristan arrived at the docks just after sunrise. Driven by the grey-haired Māori, the Black Arrows' club car mounted the kerb and, ignoring various no-entry signs, went all the way up to the gangway of the *Aotera,* a small inter-island trading vessel tied up in a remote part of Auckland Harbour.

'Here we are, guys,' said the Māori cheerfully. 'I'll introduce you to the captain. Friend of mine.'

'What's that?' asked Jack. He pointed to a black van parked near the gangplank. Four men were lifting something heavy out of the back.

'What does it look like?' said the Māori.

'A coffin?' ventured Tristan, a cold shiver racing down his spine.

'He's coming with us?' said Jack, looking incredulous.

'Perfect timing. Ship only goes once every two weeks. He's going home for burial,' said the Māori as the four men carried the Bone Scraper's coffin slowly up the gangway.

Named after a legendary Māori war canoe, the *Aotera* had seen better days. Some would have called it an unseaworthy rust bucket, but looks can be deceptive. For several decades, the *Aotera* had been ploughing the rough seas of the South Pacific, delivering supplies to the Chatham Islands.

'Just in time,' said the captain, a burly Māori with a weather-beaten face like creased leather, waiting at the top of the gangplank. 'We're about to leave. The sooner the better if we want to outrun the storm coming in from the north. Otherwise, we could be stuck here for days. Let me show you to your cabin; come on.'

Great, thought Jack as he followed the captain down some narrow stairs leading into the labyrinthine bowels of the ship, which smelled of engine oil and bunker fuel. Riding out a storm in this wasn't exactly what he'd had in mind.

'Home for the next two days or so,' said Jack. 'It's about a thousand kilometres as the crow flies.' He threw his duffel bag on the narrow bottom bunk, and peered out of the small porthole. 'Wind's up. Looks ominous and rough already. I think we're in for quite a ride, mate. You take the top one. Do you mind?'

'Not at all,' said Tristan. 'Thanks, Jack.'

'What for?'

'For coming along. No questions asked.'

'Come on, Tristan, you know me better than that. I wouldn't miss this for the world. After all, according to some, I'm an adventure junkie, right?' said Jack, trying to introduce some levity into the otherwise tense situation.

'Thanks, anyway. I know that wasn't the only reason.'

'No, it wasn't. I wasn't going to let you go halfway around the world and face all this on your own.'

Tristan nodded. 'I meant to ask you something ...'

'Go ahead.'

'What did the Bone Scraper mean when he referred to *Ars Moriendi*?'

'Ah, I knew you would ask me about that. *Ars Moriendi*, or *The Art of Dying*, is a Latin text composed by a Dominican friar in about 1415. It was widely read during the Middle Ages and very popular, especially after the ravages of the Black Death. Fascinated by death literature, the Wizard and the Bone Scraper both studied the text in jail and had formulated their own *Ars Moriendi* rules. They even made a pact to follow them to the letter.'

'The Bone Scraper told you this?'

'Yes, he did.'

'I see; and did they?' said Tristan.

Jack shrugged but didn't reply. After that, Tristan didn't pursue the matter further.

As soon as the *Aotera* left Auckland Harbour and turned south, it encountered foul weather. The seas were mountainous, making the ship pitch and roll alarmingly.

As Jack and Tristan had been told to stay in their cabin until further notice and tie themselves into their bunks if things got too rough, there

38

was no other option but to ride out the storm in the tiny, claustrophobic cabin, which only amplified the rising and falling of the bow and stern of the ship, without stabilisers to speak of. Fortunately, neither Jack nor Tristan were seasick and soon the conversation turned to how Tristan's father, the Wizard, died.

'The Bone Scraper also said,' began Tristan after a while, 'that you were there when the Wizard was dying.' Tristan never referred to the Wizard as his father.

Jack took a deep breath. He realised the moment he had been dreading for years had now arrived. The setting – being confined to a tiny cabin on an old, dilapidated vessel riding into a storm, with a coffin on board – seemed strangely appropriate for such a painful subject. He was about to tell someone he loved dearly how his father had been killed by the very man who was travelling with them in a coffin somewhere in the cargo hold.

And if that wasn't enough, Tristan was now sporting a dead man's facial tattoo on the right side of his face for the whole world to see. The irony of the situation wasn't lost on Jack, but he realised the only way to deal with the subject was to be brutally honest and meet it head on. Tristan deserved to know the truth.

Jack traced the scar on his right temple with the tips of his fingers – a reminder of that fateful night he had almost been killed – and locked eyes with Tristan, watching him intently.

'When I arrived at the Wolf's Lair – an abandoned church used by the Wizards as their clubhouse – via a secret underground passage your mother had told us about,' said Jack softly, 'this is what I found ...'

* * *

Wolf's Lair: 9 March 2010, 2:30 am

Jack could hear the chanting well before he reached the rusty door at the end of the tunnel. Faint at first, but growing louder with every step. The door was ajar, its hinges twisted to one side. Jack squeezed through and stopped. The chanting was coming from above.

'Ka mate, ka mate! Ka ora! Ka ora ...'

Walking slowly up the stairs leading from the tiny strongroom – which was once a family vault – to the crypt above, Jack tried to make sense of the strange chorus. It sounded warlike, threatening, yet strangely familiar. *The* haka, he thought, *that's it!* Just like the beginning of an All Blacks rugby game.

When he reached the top of the stairs and looked into the crypt, he almost tripped over something lying on the floor. He stepped back quickly, only to find himself standing in a pool of blood next to the Undertaker's twisted body.

The chanting became louder and more urgent.

'Tenei te tangata puhuruhuru ...'

As Jack stepped over the body, he saw the backs of six huge men standing in a semicircle in the middle of the crypt. With their arms raised and stamping their feet in rhythmic unison, they were chanting at something he couldn't quite make out. Jack moved a little to one side, and gasped.

The Wizard teetered on tiptoe on a skull the size of a large watermelon, blood dripping down his naked chest from a gaping wound at the throat. With his hands handcuffed behind his back and his ankles tied together with rope, it seemed an impossible balancing act. What Jack couldn't see in the gloom was the noose made of fine piano wire around the Wizard's neck, and the hook in the ceiling to which the wire was attached. The only reason the Wizard wasn't dead yet was because he was able to support his weight on the skull – just.

As his eyes became accustomed to the candlelight, Jack noticed something was trickling out of the eye sockets and nose of the skull. *Looks like sand,* he thought. The skull, carved out of wood, was a copy of an ingenious device invented for the Inquisition – a hanging-stool with a sinister twist. Hollow inside, it could be filled with sand from the top. Once it was full, a small, round piece of wood could be placed on top like a lid. But the lid was smaller than the opening and as the sand ran out, the lid would sink into the skull. The eyes and nose were blocked by marbles, which could be removed to let the sand trickle out, giving the executioner many options. The Wizard stood on a deadly hourglass, suspended between life and death.

Despite the gaping wound in his chest, the Undertaker, the Wizard's sergeant-at-arms, was still alive! Eyes wide open, he was staring at the gun – tantalisingly close – lying next to him on the floor. Slowly, his fingers began to move forward. Jack stood directly in front of him, mesmerised by the dance of death. The Undertaker knew what had to happen: he was going to shoot the messenger responsible for this disaster.

With white stars beginning to dance in front of his eyes and his stiff fingers refusing to obey, the Undertaker was about to give up, when suddenly he could feel it: steel – cold and reassuring – reviving his fingertips. Because it was covered in blood, the gun was slippery and he had to try several times to get a grip on it. Barely able to breathe, he closed his eyes, as the strange chanting assaulted his exhausted brain.

'Ka mate, ka mate! Ka ora ...'

You can do it, he thought. He's right in front of you. Despite life oozing out of the mortal wound, one last bit of strength remained. The Undertaker opened his eyes and raised the gun. Squinting, he took aim and fired. Because his hand had been shaking, the bullet only grazed Jack's right temple.

Dazed and with the gunshot still ringing in his ears, Jack spun around. The Bone Scraper standing directly in front of him did the same. Pulling a gun out of his belt, the Bone Scraper fired two shots at the Undertaker, lying on the floor. Jack looked down and saw the Undertaker's head blown away.

'That was close,' said the Bone Scraper, checking his gun. 'Let me have a look.'

'It's nothing, just a scratch.'

'You're a lucky guy! A little to the left and ...'

Jack pulled a handkerchief out of his pocket and pressed it against his bleeding temple.

'I did warn you,' said the Bone Scraper.

'You did. Thanks. You saved my life.'

The Bone Scraper pointed to the Wizard. 'You gave us this ...' he said.

'That's some retribution,' said Jack quietly.

'He deserves it.' The Bone Scraper looked anxious: to interrupt the *haka* was bad luck. 'You've seen it. Now, please leave. We have unfinished business here.'

Jack realised this was an order, not a request. The Bone Scraper's radio began to crackle. One of his scouts was reporting in.

'The cops just passed the roundabout,' announced the Bone Scraper. 'We have ten minutes.' Without saying another word, he turned around and began to chant:

'Kikiki kakaka kauana! Kei waniwania taku taraKei tarawahia, kei to rua i te kerokero!'

Careful not to step in the bloody mess, Jack walked around the Undertaker's body and hurried down the stairs and into the strong-room below.

'Ka mate, ka mate! Ka ora! Ka ora!' chanted the Warriors behind him.

With the adrenaline rush ebbing, elation gave way to panic. Dashing through the tunnel, his head throbbing with pain, Jack had only one thing on his mind: to get away. As he reached the outside, he took a deep breath and wondered if the Wizard was still alive.

* * *

'You didn't actually see him die, did you?' asked Tristan after Jack had finished. He had to shout to make himself heard, as the howling wind and the rain drumming against the porthole were too loud and the rolling ship made sitting on the spartan bunk uncomfortable.

'No. I told you all I saw.'

'This was all part of *Ars Moriendi* then, do you think?'

'In a strange way, perhaps yes, it was.'

'Like a pact between two friends who were close once, but had grown apart?'

'I suppose you could say that, but there was a lot more to all this.'

Tristan nodded. 'I never actually met my father, you know. The picture I have of him in my mind has been cobbled together from what others had said about him, and that includes you, Jack. You know more about my father than I do. Don't you think that's strange?'

'It is, but he was a strange man, and these were exceptional circumstances and troubled times.'

'Many said he was evil, and that included my mother. She was terrified of him, both physically and spiritually. Did he affect you in that way?'

Jack took his time before replying. He was desperately searching for the right way to answer this emotionally charged question, with potentially far-reaching consequences for a young man searching for his identity and place in the world.

Jack understood better than most what Tristan was going through, as he had been there himself. Often searching for answers that weren't there. He didn't want his friend and protégé to experience the same pain and disappointment.

'Evil is something we create; a path of choice some follow. It isn't something you inherit or are born with. It's a choice often triggered by temptation. Ambition, greed, pride, jealousy. But a choice, nevertheless.'

'You really believe that?'

'I do.'

Obviously relieved, Tristan sat back. 'I can't tell you what hearing this means to me. Especially coming from you.'

'I think I can,' said Jack, feeling a heavy burden lifting from his soul. 'We are not responsible for the actions of those who have gone before us. We can only learn from them and follow our own path. You of all people know this, Tristan. Your gift is one you must treasure.'

'I do. I can feel what we're doing here, right now, is part of that. I can clearly see the path I must follow, and I can't tell you how grateful I am that you are here to walk it with me and show me the way.'

'We are but instruments of destiny and fate, Tristan. Once we understand that, everything falls into place. Trust me.'

'I do. I think I'm now ready to meet the grandmother I didn't know I had.'

Feeling suddenly exhausted, Tristan lay down on his bunk, closed his eyes and, despite the violent pitching of the ship and the howling wind outside, drifted into a deep sleep. It was the way his mind dealt with an emotional struggle that had been building for years and had just reached its climax.

Smiling, Jack reached for the rough blanket at the foot of the bunk and draped it tenderly over Tristan.

Waitangi, Chatham Islands: 26 September

A dense sea mist hovered over the port of Waitangi like a shroud as the *Aotera* sailed into the safety of the harbour after a particularly rough crossing from Auckland.

'How do you feel?' asked Jack, standing on deck next to Tristan. It was early morning and both of them had blankets draped over their shoulders to keep warm, but they had been up for hours, watching the Chatham Islands rise out of the ominous storm clouds on the horizon.

'Mixed feelings, as you would expect, but thanks to you, a sense of calmness and anticipation, nevertheless.'

Tristan pointed to the shore. 'I wonder what's waiting for me here in this remote, isolated place? After all, this is where my ancestors come from. In a strange way, I belong here.'

As the ship was slowly approaching the wharf, Jack could see a group of people watching them from the shore. Helped by two men waiting on the wharf, it didn't take the crew long to dock and lower the gangplank.

The captain stepped out of the wheelhouse and walked over to Tristan and Jack. 'Welcome to Waitangi,' he said. 'Wasn't too bad after all. I've seen a lot worse.'

'If you say so,' replied Jack, who had barely slept in two days and was massaging his aching neck. 'What now?'

The captain pointed to a small procession of a dozen or so people walking along the wharf. 'Watch,' he said.

One person in particular stood out: a tall, elderly woman wearing a strange-looking cloak, her long, striking white hair like an ethereal beacon breaking the monotony of the grey morning.

Supported by a young woman and a walking stick, she walked up to the gangplank and looked up at the captain watching her from above. 'I've come to collect my son,' she said, her voice strong and melodious.

'Everything is ready, Kiri Te Papatahi,' said the captain.

The woman nodded, turned around, and spoke to a group of men standing behind her. Moments later, six young men, all Māori, stepped forward and came walking up the gangplank.

'My grandmother,' said Tristan, choking with emotion.

Jack put his arm around him and held him tight, bracing himself for what he knew was about to come.

The six men went below deck and returned a short time later carrying the Bone Scraper's coffin. Meanwhile, the crew had assembled on deck and were watching.

As soon as Kiri Te Papatahi saw the coffin appear at the top of the gangplank, she raised her hands and began to chant *Me tangi, kāpā ko te mate i te marama'* , as the men began to slowly walk down the gangplank.

The captain turned to Tristan. 'You should follow them,' he said. 'It's the right way.'

Tristan nodded and fell in behind the pallbearers.

As the pallbearers reached the bottom of the gangplank, Kiri Te Papatahi placed her right hand on her son's coffin and closed her eyes. A heartbroken mother was greeting her dead son and taking him home. It was an intensely moving moment, affecting all present.

Wearing a traditional *korowai* cloak woven with feathers – a tasselled mantle of honour and great cultural meaning – and a wreath of *kawakawa* leaves on her head – a plant of spiritual significance and a sign of mourning – Kiri Te Papatahi looked almost regal despite her advanced years and obvious frailties.

The *korowai* was a *taonga*, a treasure, which had been in her family for generations and represented her lineage and tribal affiliations.

Slowly, the mourning mother withdrew her hand and looked at Tristan standing behind the coffin. 'Tristan?' she asked, her voice quavering with emotion.

Tristan nodded.

'Come, walk with me. We are taking him home. It isn't far. I live just over there.'

'This is Jack Rogan, a close friend,' said Tristan and pointed to Jack standing behind him.

Kiri Te Papatahi looked at Jack, a hesitant smile spreading across her wan face. 'Ah. The storyteller. Welcome, Mr Rogan. I know who you are. My son told me a lot about you.'

Kiri Te Papatahi held out her arm. 'Come, please walk with me as well. I need all the support I can get.'

'I'm honoured,' said Jack.

As the little procession left the wharf and turned into the street, it began to rain. *The heavens are weeping,* thought Jack. *How appropriate.*

Ignoring the rain, people came from all over and lined the footpath like a spontaneous guard of honour. It wasn't curiosity that brought them, but respect.

Holding Tristan's elbow with one hand, and Jack's arm with the other, Kiri Te Papatahi followed her son's coffin on its final journey. She was looking forward to getting to know her only grandchild, as one generation passed into the afterlife, and the next emerged to keep the ancestral flame burning and tribal memory alive.

The Funeral, Waitangi: 28 September

I The Promise

The Bone Scraper's Funeral, the *tangi*, lasted for three days, with most of the traditional Māori rites and customs, the *tangihanga*, taking place in Kiri Te Papatahi's modest home, which stood on the site of the very first tribal *marae*, meeting ground, erected shortly after the island invasion in 1835.

The Bone Scraper's coffin was open, as tradition demanded, to allow the mourners to say farewell and talk to the deceased, as was customary. Jack and Tristan were staying in the house as honoured guests and Tristan, in particular, was viewed not only with curiosity but also with respect.

His grandmother used this precious time to get to know her grandson and had many conversations with him. Jack used the time to talk to the locals, especially the elders, to learn more about Māori history and culture. He was particularly interested in stories about the *Mokomokai*, the trade of Māori heads for muskets, which had played such an important part in the devastating Musket Wars.

At the end of the last day of the funeral, Kiri Te Papatahi asked Tristan and Jack to see her in private after all the mourners had left.

'Any idea what this is all about?' asked Jack as they made their way to the back of the house, where the body was on display.

'I think it's about the missing head. It hasn't been talked about much so far and I had many conversations with my grandmother. And besides, we are leaving tomorrow.'

'Makes sense. Let's see if you're right.'

Sitting by herself next to her son's open coffin, the traditional *korowai* cloak draped over her shoulders, Kiri Te Papatahi looked up as Jack and Tristan walked in.

'Please come and sit with me,' she said and pointed to some chairs lined up along the wall.

'Firstly, I wanted to thank you both for coming all the way from Europe to see my son before he died. I know it meant a great deal to him, just as you being here and attending his funeral means a great deal to me.'

Kiri Te Papatahi turned to face Tristan sitting opposite.

'You told me that you made a promise just before my son died?'

'Yes, I did,' said Tristan. 'I promised to try to find the missing head of Parema Te Pahau, who was killed here in battle in 1840. I understand that his head was cut off by the victors and kept as a trophy – until it disappeared.'

'That's correct as far as it goes, but of course, there's a lot more to all this.'

'I did suspect that. Your son – my uncle – suggested that I should talk to you about this, as you may be able to help me fulfil my promise. Apparently, you know more about this matter than he ever did.'

Kiri Te Papatahi pointed to the coffin next to her. 'He made a similar promise when his father died many years ago. He was still a boy at the time and I suspect that he didn't fully understand what it all meant. A troubled youth, he left the island just before he turned eighteen and never returned.'

Kiri Te Papatahi looked sadly at the coffin. 'What we do know is that he was unable to keep his promise and turned to you, the youngest surviving member of our line, just before he died, and passed the burden of the promise to you.'

'Yes, that's what happened.'

'And your new *moko* tells me that you accepted and agreed; correct?'

Tristan nodded.

'Very noble of you. But then, you are no ordinary young man, are you?'

'I don't know what you mean.'

'Oh, I think you do; isn't that right, Mr Rogan?'

'There is nothing ordinary about Tristan,' said Jack. 'In fact, he's the most extraordinary young man I've come across. He can hear the whisper of angels and glimpse eternity,' added Jack softly.

'You put it beautifully, just like one would expect from a writer of your standing. Yes, he's extraordinary, because he has inherited the gift from his mother. She in turn, inherited it from her grandmother. Somehow, I missed out altogether.' Kiri Te Papatahi waved dismissively. 'Just as well. This gift is both a blessing and a burden, as you would be well aware, Tristan.'

Tristan nodded.

'Then again, this isn't a matter of choice. The only choice you have is in how you use this gift.'

'That's true,' said Tristan, sensing the right moment had arrived to talk to his grandmother about the missing head. He had hesitated to ask her about it earlier, as that could have appeared insensitive, perhaps even offensive, in the circumstances.

'Do you know what happened to Parema Te Pahau's head?' asked Tristan, meeting the subject head on.

Kiri Te Papatahi nodded. 'Up to a point. But first, let me tell you something about the man. Apart from being a great leader and feared warrior, he was a *tohunga matakite*, a revered foreteller of the future. But that wasn't all. Legend has it that he was able to communicate with Hine-nui-te-pō, the goddess of death and the underworld, who receives the spirits of the dead when they die. He was famous for that and had a unique full-face *moko*, a *pūkanohi*, which was a visual expression of his power and prestige.'

Kiri Te Papatahi pointed to Tristan. 'I can see that you are now wearing a partial *pūkanohi* on the right side of your face. Just as my son here had done since he made that fateful promise after his father died. But as I just said, the *moko* isn't complete, or even accurate, but only part of Parema Te Pahau's famous *pūkanohi*. That's the problem ... one of them.'

'How come?' asked Jack.

'My son was very affected by his father's death and took the promise he made very seriously. So much so, that he took the name Parema Te Pahau, and the *moko* we just talked about is directly related to the search for the head. But before I tell you more, let me tell you what happened to the famous chief's head.'

II Parema Te Pahau's Missing Head

Kiri Te Papatahi turned towards the open coffin and began to address her dead son directly: 'Remember, you came to me the day after your father died and asked me about Parema Te Pahau's head? I told you that it had been traded by Ngāti Tama for muskets, after it had been preserved in the traditional way.'

'*Mokomokai?*' said Jack.

'Exactly,' said Kiri Te Papatahi. 'That's what these heads were called. Do you know how they were preserved?'

'Yes. I spoke to a few of the elders here about this and they told me. First, the brain and the eyes were removed, just as the Egyptians had done when preparing their mummies. After that, the orifices were sealed with flax fibre and gum, the head was then boiled and smoked over an open fire before being dried for several days in the sun. Finally, it was covered in shark oil. This procedure was very effective and preserved the head for years, if not indefinitely. These heads were very sought-after by Europeans, who traded them for muskets, and then sold them on at enormous profit to museums and collectors as exotic curios from the Antipodes. What made these heads so special were the stunning *pūkanohi*, the tattoos.'

'And is this what happened to Parema Te Pahau's head?' asked Tristan.

'Yes,' said his grandmother.

'As I understand it, each of these tattoos was unique and only men had full-facial *moko*, denoting high social status and showing tribal connections to ancestors. That's correct, isn't it?' said Tristan.

'Yes.' Kiri Te Papatahi pointed to her own striking *moko* on her chin. 'Women have *moko* just like mine, but never full *moko*. That is strictly the province of men, especially famous warriors and chiefs.'

Then she turned towards the coffin and again addressed her son.

'You became obsessed with finding Parema Te Pahau's head and fulfilling the promise you had made to your father, remember? So much so, that once you reached Auckland and found a job on the docks, you used all your time and money to find out all you could about it.'

51

Lost in thought, Kiri Te Papatahi paused and looked at something in the distance only she could see. 'You found out that after Parema Te Pahau was killed in battle, and his head cut off and embalmed, it was traded for muskets in 1842, and taken to Auckland with other *Mokomokai*. In Auckland, the trail went cold until you came across a famous book – *Moko; or Māori Tattooing* by Major General Horatio Robley, published in 1896.' Kiri Te Papatahi turned to face her grandson. 'Have you heard of Robley, Tristan?'

Tristan shook his head.

'I have,' said Jack. 'Your son told me about him during one of our interviews. Robley was a British officer who fought in nineteenth-century colonial wars in New Zealand. He fought in the Battle of Gate Pā in 1864, which resulted in a devastating defeat of the British forces in the New Zealand Wars. But he was also an artist, collector and author, and during his time in New Zealand, he became very interested in Māori culture, especially tattooing, and completed numerous sketches of tattoos of dead or wounded Māori warriors. These sketches were later published in the *Illustrated London News*.'

'Very good, Mr Rogan, but Robley is best known for something else: his collection of *Mokomokai*. After the book's publication, Robley built up a large collection of more than thirty-five Māori heads, which he acquired over several years. Records kept in the Auckland Institute and Museum show that one of those heads, the most famous one, was most likely that of Parema Te Pahau.'

Kiri Te Papatahi turned towards her son's coffin once again. 'You told me about that, remember? You were very disappointed because it looked like the end of your search for the head and in some way, it was just that. You had reached a dead end, or so you thought at the time. That's when you came across an unexpected piece of information, which kept the search alive.'

By now, Jack had pulled out his notebook and was taking notes. 'What kind of information?' he asked.

'A sketch by Charles Goldie, one of New Zealand's most acclaimed painters. He is best known for his striking portraits of tattooed Māori chiefs and leaders. One of those sketches was a study for a bigger work, a portrait of – wait for it – Parema Te Pahau.'

'How is that possible?' said Tristan. 'Parema Te Pahau died in battle in 1840.'

'Ah. That's the intriguing part about all this. It would appear that Goldie had access to the mummified head, because the sketch makes that very clear. He was interested in the unique *moko* and for some reason, the sketch only shows the right side of the dead warrior's face.'

'Just to be clear,' said Jack, pointing to the notebook with his pencil. 'After Parema Te Pahau's mummified head was traded for muskets here on the Chatham Islands, it was taken to Auckland with other *Mokomokai* by traders who had acquired them from the locals here in return for muskets. In Auckland, the trail went cold, until your son came across a book about Māori tattooing by Major General Robley, published in London in 1896. This revived the search for the missing head and resulted in a significant discovery: Apparently, Robley began collecting *Mokomokai* after the publication of his book, and over several years built up a large collection of about thirty-five *Mokomokai*, one of which appears to have been the head of Parema Te Pahau. Am I correct?'

Kiri Te Papatahi looked at Jack and nodded. 'Yes, you are.'

'What about that Goldie sketch?' asked Tristan. 'How is this relevant here?'

'You are wearing it on your face, Tristan. Somehow, my son found this sketch in the art gallery records and had the Parema Te Pahau *moko* drawn by Goldie tattooed on the right side of his face, just as it was depicted in the sketch, as this appeared to be the only surviving image of Parema Te Pahau's *moko*.'

'Why did he do that?' said Jack, shaking his head.

'Mainly out of respect, but there was another reason. He thought it would help him identify the head should it be found one day. You could hardly expect the *Mokomokai* to have nametags, could you?'

Jack nodded. 'That was clever, but that was the end of the search then, right?'

'As far as my son was concerned, yes. Soon after all this, he went to Australia, and his younger brother, Joe, and his sister – your mother, Tristan – followed him soon after. All bright young folk left the islands, as there were few opportunities to make a life here. In Sydney, they met Eugene, joined his family circus, and became the Flying Kiwis. You know the rest,' said Kiri Te Papatahi sadly, as she remembered the tragic consequences of that fateful decision.

Jack closed his notebook. 'That's it then, I suppose?' he said.

'Not quite,' said Kiri Te Papatahi, a faint smile appearing on her face. 'It may have been the end of the search as far as my son was concerned, but for me, it was just the beginning.'

'What do you mean?' said Tristan.

'I took over.'

'In what way?' asked Jack, surprised.

'We may live in a remote part of the world here, Mr Rogan, but we are by no means isolated. We have excellent internet services here and, as you obviously know, once you have that, you are connected to the world. I joined forces with other like-minded women here on the island, and we began a campaign.'

'What kind of campaign?' said Jack, wondering where this was going.

'A campaign for the retrieval and repatriation of Māori remains kept in museums and collections around the world.'

'Seriously?' said Tristan.

'Yes, and I'm pleased to tell you that we have been very successful in this. In 1990, we were instrumental in having a New Zealand Government programme called Karanga Aotearoa enacted for the repatriation of Māori remains. In 2016, the Smithsonian returned its Māori remains, together with four mummified heads. More recently, London's Natural History Museum and the Natural History Museum in Vienna have also successfully repatriated remains.'

'And I suppose you also campaigned for the return of the Robley *Mokomokai* collection?' said Jack, a twinkle in his eyes.

'Yes, of course. That was certainly one of the main drivers of all this, as far as I was concerned. I saw it as a way of locating Parema Te

Pahau's head and bringing it home, should it turn out it was in fact part of the Robley collection, as the information obtained by my son seemed to suggest.'

Impressed, Jack opened his notebook again.

'Do you know what happened to the collection?' he asked.

'I do. In 1908, Robley offered it to the New Zealand Government, but the offer was declined. It was eventually purchased by the American Museum of Natural History in New York—'

'And is the collection still there?' interjected Jack.

'No. The collection was repatriated in 2014 as part of the Karanga Aotearoa Programme I mentioned, and is now in the Te Papa Tongarewa Museum in Wellington.'

'Then we do know where the head is, don't we?' ventured Tristan.

'Unfortunately, no.'

'Oh? How come?' said Jack.

'Because Robley kept the five best heads for himself, and this apparently included the head of Parema Te Pahau.'

'I see,' said Jack, noting the dejection in Kiri Te Papatahi's voice. 'Do we know what happened to them?'

'They vanished after Robley died in 1930, just as my son is about to vanish from the stage of life.'

Kiri Te Papatahi stood up, leaned over the coffin and tenderly touched her son's tattooed face with the tips of her fingers. Then she closed the lid of the coffin and turned around. 'But you, Tristan, can make sure that he is not forgotten. If anyone can find Parema Te Pahau's head and bring it home for burial, you can. And if you do, Parema Te Pahau will join his ancestors in the afterlife, and his awesome occult powers will pass to you. I only hope that I live to see that happen.'

'Two days of misery getting here, and two hours in a comfortable plane getting back. I know which I prefer,' said Jack, as they were boarding the plane to Auckland early the next morning.

'So do I,' said Tristan. 'Have you given some thought to where we go with this from here?'

'Sure have. I can't wait to see the Goldie portraits in the art gallery in Auckland and talk to the curator about that sketch.'

'My thoughts exactly. We can't disappoint my grandmother now, can we?'

'No, we can't,' said Jack, enjoying the familiar adventure rush making the fine hairs on the back of his neck tingle with excitement.

Auckland Art Gallery: 29 September

Jack pointed to one of Goldie's paintings on display – *Reverie* – *Pipi Haerehuka* – *Chieftainess of the Arawa Tribe* – and turned to Tristan standing next to him.

'Don't you think she looks like your grandmother?'

'Does a bit,' conceded Tristan. 'Stunning painting.'

'It was a gift by the artist to the art gallery in 1939, in memory of his mother,' said the curator, who had just walked in and overheard the remark. 'You wanted to see me? I'm sorry to keep you waiting.'

Jack spun around and looked at the young woman smiling at him. 'Yes. Thank you,' he said. 'This gallery is quite something.'

'It is. Goldie and Lindauer, two of New Zealand's most eminent painters, especially as far as Māori portraits are concerned, all on display in one room. I understand that's what brings you here, Mr Rogan? How can I be of assistance?'

'This is Tristan Te Papatahi, grandson of Kiri Te Papatahi, who lives on the Chatham Islands. We've just come from there. Funeral … her son.'

'I'm sorry.' If the curator was at all surprised by Tristan's striking *moko*, she didn't show it.

'Would I be right in saying that Kiri Te Papatahi is no stranger to you?' said Jack.

'Certainly not. What she has done for repatriating Māori remains and creating awareness of Māori culture, both here and overseas, is remarkable.'

'What brings us here,' continued Jack, 'is part of that very same process. Tristan is trying to locate the remains of one of his ancestors. A *Mokomokai*, the mummified head of Parema Te Pahau, a famous warrior killed on the Chatham Islands in 1840, to be precise.'

'How intriguing. And you think that I can help?'

'Yes, we hope so.' Jack pointed to the Goldie painting he had just admired. 'Because it all has to do with Goldie. One of his sketches, to be precise.'

'Fascinating. Let's go into my office. We can talk more freely there.'

After Jack had explained the possible connection between Goldie's work and Parema Te Papatahi's *moko*, and how the Bone Scraper appeared to have somehow gained access to the Goldie sketch and used it as a template for his *moko*, the curator asked her assistant to retrieve Goldie's manuscript notes and sketchbook from the archives.

'Well, here we are. Let's see.' The curator put on some white gloves and opened the sketchbook. It didn't take her long to find what she was looking for. 'Have a look at this, gentlemen. Is that what you're after?' She turned the sketchbook around and showed it to Tristan, who kept staring at the page, his eyes wide with astonishment.

The drawing, in pencil, showed the right side of a Māori head that had been severed at the neck. The eye was closed, the mouth partially open with the teeth exposed. The long, thick, black hair tied into a knot at the top had two feathers threaded through it. But most striking of all was the intricate *moko*, depicted in detail and the obvious focal point of the drawing.

Jack's eyes went straight to the notation in Goldie's distinctive handwriting, below the head: *Chief Parema Te Pahau. Killed in battle 1840, Chatham Islands.*

Tristan traced his *moko* with his fingertips and continued to stare at the sketch in front of him.

'It's very similar to yours, but not the same,' said Jack. 'I wonder why?'

'There could be numerous explanations for this. This sketchbook of pencil drawings was given by Goldie to one of his friends, Frank Pullen. It was deposited with the gallery here in about 1955 by Pullen's brother. It's been in our archives ever since.'

'According to Tristan's grandmother, his uncle had his face tattooed here in Auckland, where he lived in about 1990. We have no idea how he found out about the sketch, or how he managed to gain access to it. No matter, his *moko* was at least somehow "inspired" by the drawing. So much is obvious.'

'He or the tattooist must have seen the sketch here in our archives. That's certainly possible. Perhaps a drawing was made of the design and later used for the *moko*?' ventured the curator.

'Could be,' said Jack.

Noticing the disappointment in his voice, the curator reached for Goldie's manuscript notes and looked at Jack. 'But wait, there's more,' she said, smiling.

'There is?' said Tristan.

'Yes. Goldie was very meticulous and kept detailed records of his subjects and work generally. His handwritten notes are fascinating and reveal a lot about the man. Ah, here it is,' said the curator and held up a faded page covered in Goldie's spidery handwriting. 'These notes here suggest that Goldie actually painted a portrait of Parema Te Pahau shortly after he made the sketch—'

'*Really?*' said Jack, feeling a rush of anticipation.

'Yes, and I can tell you something about it you may find useful.'

'You can?' said Tristan, sensing something strange reaching out of the past.

'It happened a few years ago. I was an assistant to the then curator at the time. We were approached by a solicitor acting for an estate, indicating that a Goldie painting of a Māori warrior had been left to the art gallery. Naturally, we were very excited and curious about this and made an appointment with the solicitor to see it. As it happened, his office was just down the road from here.'

The curator paused and stared at the sketch in front of her as she remembered the meeting.

'And?' prompted Jack.

'It was magnificent. One of Goldie's best. It was a portrait of Parema Te Pahau, painted in 1903.'

Stunned silence.

'How could that be?' asked Tristan softly after a while. 'Parema Te Pahau died in 1840.'

The curator pointed to Goldie's manuscript notes. 'Goldie tells us how right here. He used the mummified head as his subject and brought the famous Māori warrior chief back to life, with particular attention to his magnificent *moko*—'

'Which means that he must have had access to the head at the time he painted the portrait,' said Tristan.

'No doubt about it, because the portrait showed the entire *moko* in detail seen from the front, not like the sketch, which only shows one side of the face.'

'Incredible! What happened to the painting?' asked Jack, 'Do you know? It's obviously not here.'

'Unfortunately, no. The will was contested, and the bequest to the gallery was set aside and failed.'

'Do you know what happened to the painting after that?' said Tristan.

'It was sold at auction. The gallery tried to buy it, but couldn't raise the money. We lost sight of it after that. Another national treasure lost,' said the curator, the frustration in her voice apparent.

'You wouldn't perchance have a picture of it, would you?' asked Jack, clutching at straws.

The curator shook her head. 'But I can tell you who sold it. Local auctioneers right here in Auckland. They sold a number of Goldie's paintings over the years. Who knows; they might still have records of the sale? I can give you their address if you like.'

'Thank you. That would be most helpful,' said Jack.

'What do you think?' said Tristan as they were leaving the gallery.

'We achieved quite a bit today, wouldn't you say?' said Jack, forever the optimist. 'At least the *Mokomokai* trail hasn't gone cold; it's still warm. What do you reckon?'

Tristan nodded. 'So, what's next?'

'As I see it, we have two main issues here: First, we have to find the head, if it's still around somewhere, that is. That's obvious. We know that there are hundreds of *Mokomokai* in museums and private collections around the world. In order to find your ancestor's head, we must be able to identify it, right?'

'Of course.'

'We now know that your *moko* here will not be enough to do that. We need more. We need the Goldie portrait, because it is a faithful representation of Parema Te Pahau's unique *moko*. In short, we need the portrait, because without it, we can't be sure the head is the right one, even if we find one that looks like it.'

'Of course not. So, what's next?'

'Portrait first, head later. And besides, I think we have a better chance of finding the portrait than the head, this early in our search.'

'True.'

'So, next is a visit to the auctioneers; what else?'

'You're enjoying this, aren't you?' said Tristan.

'What do you think? I had no idea New Zealand could be this much fun, mate. Wasn't she cute?'

'Who?'

'The curator. Smart girl, and so helpful.'

'I don't know what it is with you and women,' said Tristan, shaking his head. 'I saw the way she looked at you. Even my grandmother—'

'What are you talking about?'

'Never mind.' *Incorrigible rascal*, thought Tristan, grinning from ear to ear, but wisely holding his tongue.

Hamish McNamara & Sons Auctioneers, Auckland: 29 September

The auctioneers whom Jack and Tristan were looking for had occupied the same historical building on Karangahape Road in Auckland for almost a hundred years, but since the advent of online auctions, business had declined considerably.

To a large extent this was because Donald McNamara, the current owner, had no-one to take over the family business and due to his advanced years, he was not very computer savvy.

Apart from being old-school fine art auctioneers, Hamish McNamara & Sons had recently branched out into the antiquarian business, selling fine prints, lithographs and curios, mainly of New Zealand or Māori origin, in an attempt to keep the family business afloat.

A well-dressed elderly lady standing behind the counter looked up as Jack and Tristan walked in. She took off her reading glasses and was sizing up Jack with interest. 'May I help you, gentlemen?' she asked, echoes of her Scottish origin detectable beneath her heavy New Zealand accent.

'We have just been to the art gallery and were admiring Charles Goldie's paintings,' said Jack, giving the lady his best smile, 'and we have been referred to you by the curator.'

'Ah. Stunning, aren't they? If you are after a Goldie, I must disappoint you, I'm afraid. They rarely come up for sale and besides, the prices have gone through the roof,' said the lady behind the counter, a sparkle in her eyes.

'Actually, we're interested in a Goldie you sold a few years ago. A portrait of Parema Te Pahau, a Māori chief killed in battle on the Chatham Islands in 1840.'

The lady looked at Jack and, judging by her expression, this was something she hadn't expected. 'I remember that sale well. It broke all records at the time. It was also our last sale of a Goldie,' she added.

'You better talk to my brother about this. Please wait here; I'll get him. May I ask who——?'

'Jack Rogan,' replied Jack casually.

'Ah,' said the lady, smiling.

A few minutes later, a side door opened and Donald McNamara swept into the room, followed by his sister. Impeccably dressed in a three-piece suit, white shirt and bow tie, his white hair neatly parted in the middle, he walked straight up to Jack and held out his hand. 'Would you perhaps be the Jack Rogan who found Tchaikovsky's lost symphony a few years ago, and returned it to St Petersburg?'

'I am,' said Jack, surprised, and shook hands with McNamara.

'My sister recognised you. She has read all of your books; haven't you, my dear?'

Jack smiled, obviously pleased to have been recognised.

Tristan rolled his eyes and looked up at the ceiling.

'My goodness, how incredible! Tchaikovsky is one of my favourite composers and I have followed the discovery of the lost symphony with great interest. What a story! We even watched the premiere of the symphony in St Petersburg on TV, didn't we, Ayleen?' said McNamara, addressing his sister. 'What brings you to my humble establishment, Mr Rogan?'

'It's quite a story,' said Jack.

'Then please step into my office and you can tell me all about it.'

As soon as Jack entered the spacious, wood-panelled room smelling of furniture polish and cigar smoke, he had the distinct feeling of travelling back in time. Being keenly interested in antiques, his eyes went straight to the mahogany partners desk dominating the room, and then drifted to a beautiful secretaire and several tall bookcases, the shelves crammed with leather-bound books, and Royal Doulton toby jugs of pirates, pious monks and knights in armour staring into space.

'You have some magnificent pieces in here,' said Jack, pointing to a pair of vases on a sideboard next to an elegant longcase clock made in Glasgow. 'Moorcroft?' he asked.

'Yes, they belonged to my grandfather. He was an avid collector. This room is almost exactly as he left it, including the paintings and etchings on the walls. It seemed a shame to change anything,' said McNamara. 'And besides, we are only custodians of places like this, often for just a short time because it's always later than we think; isn't that so?'

Jack nodded.

'My father loved this room, and so do I,' continued McNamara.

'I can see why,' said Jack. 'This is a treasure trove, especially in the kind of world we live in now,' said Jack. 'Memories frozen in time.'

'How right you are, Mr Rogan. So, what brings you here?'

McNamara pointed to a faded leather Chesterfield and two chairs, facing a marble fireplace with a stunning painting of a Māori battle scene hanging above it. 'Please take a seat.'

He looks like a Russian revolutionary, thought Jack as he watched McNamara while telling the story of Parema Te Pahau's head, the connection with Tristan, and the promise he'd given to his dying uncle. Jack also explained why bringing the head back home for burial was so important.

McNamara listened, enthralled, without interrupting. He played with his bowtie, a nervous habit, but otherwise sat perfectly still, his ice-blue eyes behind gold-rimmed glasses fixed on Jack.

'We've been offered several *Mokomokai* over the years,' said McNamara after Jack had finished, 'but we refused to buy or handle the sale. Culturally, far too sensitive. Did you know that the fascination with these heads goes all the way back to Sir Joseph Banks?'

'The famous botanist who accompanied Captain Cook on the *Endeavour*?' interjected Jack.

'Yes. Apparently, he traded some linen underwear for the head of a young Māori boy. Grotesque, don't you think?'

McNamara sat back and looked at Tristan sitting opposite. 'So, why is Goldie's portrait of Parema Te Pahau so important to you, young man?' he asked.

Tristan pointed to his *moko*. 'Because of this. The portrait is the only surviving image of the chief's *moko* that we are aware of, and without knowing what it looks like, we cannot identify the head.'

'Makes sense. So, that's your interest in the painting? I suppose you are trying to find out who bought it, yes?'

'Correct,' said Jack. 'And we were hoping you would be able to help us with that.'

McNamara took off his glasses and began to polish them with a white handkerchief. 'Normally, information about buyers would be strictly confidential, but hearing your story and knowing who you are, an exception may be warranted, Mr Rogan.'

'Thank you,' said Jack, feeling relieved.

McNamara put his glasses back on, stood up, walked to his desk and took a ledger out of one of the drawers. 'Ah, here we are. I remember the auction well,' he said. 'Bidding in the auction room was spirited, but one bidder was bidding over the phone, which was quite unusual as far as we were concerned. He drove the price up and acquired the painting.'

'Can you tell us more?' said Jack.

'The bid came all the way from Japan. All I have here is a name and an address in Kyoto. The money was transferred into our bank account, and we sent the painting to the given address. All contact was over the phone. That's all I can tell you.'

'Can you give us the name and address?' asked Jack quietly.

'Yes, I will write it all down for you.'

Jack took a deep breath and locked eyes with Tristan, who smiled back in silent reply.

Kyoto, Japan: 1 October

'We can take the bullet train, the *shinkansen*. It goes from right here in the airport, as I remember it,' said Jack, trying to find his way around the busy Kansai International Airport, where all the signs were in Japanese and everyone was in a great hurry, rushing through insanely crowded corridors and following coloured lines on the ground like busy ants on a mission.

'When were you here?' asked Tristan.

'A long time ago. I spent a few days in Kyoto after one of my assignments in Afghanistan. I was going through a rough patch at the time ...'

'What kind of rough patch?'

'I had seen too much violence and death, and needed some time out.'

'Why Kyoto?'

'Zen Buddhism. I thought a little meditation in one of the monasteries would help me. An American helicopter pilot I interviewed in a field hospital suggested it. He had just lost a leg.'

'And did it? Help, I mean?'

'Yes, it did. Kyoto is amazing, as you will see. It's a spiritual place. Many say it's the soul of Japan, with hundreds of temples, some of them dating back to the eleventh century. Japan has twenty UNESCO World Cultural Heritage Sites, seventeen of which are in Kyoto, because Kyoto wasn't bombed during the war. Most of this historical city is still intact.'

'I see. Thanks for arranging the detour, by the way. I appreciate it.'

'Coming here makes sense, don't you think? Flying back to Venice from Auckland via Japan isn't much of a detour. And besides, we're in this together.'

'You're itching to find out about this mystery buyer from Kyoto, aren't you?' said Tristan, a knowing smile spreading across his face.

'You know me too well.' Jack reached into his pocket and pulled out the piece of paper McNamara had given him. 'That's all we have to go by in our search for the Goldie portrait: a name and an address. Let's knock on the door and see what happens.'

'You're in your element, aren't you, Jack?' said Tristan.

'We both are. Going to Kyoto in person is the only way we can get to the bottom of this and take the next step, right?'

'Suppose so.'

'We are almost there.' Jack pointed ahead. 'The train goes from somewhere right here. All we have to work out now is how to get a ticket out of one of these infernal machines. Everything here is automated and hardly anyone speaks English. That's quite a challenge, as you will see.'

After several attempts and much swearing, Jack had almost given up, when an elderly Japanese man who spoke a little English took pity on him and helped with the tickets. He also pointed them in the right direction to catch the train to Kyoto.

'What now?' said Tristan, being pushed along by the throng as hundreds of commuters were getting off the train in Kyoto after a breathtakingly fast trip, and were rushing to the exit.

'We catch a taxi.'

'I'm glad one of us knows what to do because I certainly don't,' said Tristan, who was getting many sideways looks because of his tattooed face. In Japan, tattoos were mainly the province of the notorious Yakuza, the traditional crime syndicates, and facial tattoos like Tristan's *moko* were a curiosity rarely seen in public.

Moved along by uniformed traffic wardens, rows of taxis were waiting in front of the railway station. Standing in orderly queues, commuters were patiently waiting their turn. When Jack's turn came, the attendant opened the boot of the taxi for Jack and Tristan to put their luggage inside.

The driver didn't get out of the cab, nor did he speak any English. Jack had been warned about this and showed the white-gloved driver a piece of paper with the address – 584 Komatsu-cho, Higashiyama-ku – written on it. The driver looked at the piece of paper, nodded, and eased his way into the heavy traffic leaving the station.

When the taxi came to a sudden halt behind a tourist bus, Jack looked out of the window. *A temple? This can't be it, surely?* he thought.

Before he could ask the taxi driver, the driver turned around. 'Kennin-ji,' he said and pointed to the temple complex buzzing with tourists.

'Do you think this is it?' asked Tristan, looking around.

'Not what I expected. Only one way to find out,' said Jack and paid the fare. 'Looks familiar. I think I've been here before. Life's full of surprises. Come on.'

Jack and Tristan followed the horde of excited tourists flocking to the entrance of Kennin-ji, the oldest Zen Buddhist temple in Kyoto.

Founded by Eisai, a monk who brought Zen to Japan from China in 1202 CE, it gradually developed into one of the largest temple complexes of the Rinzai sect. Now a major tourist attraction in Kyoto, with hundreds of visitors every day, it was best known for the Abbot's Quarters, the stunning Dharma Hall, the Tea House, and the Imperial Messenger Gate, which still bore arrow damage from ferocious wars. The huge complex comprised fourteen smaller temples within the extensive grounds, with an additional seventy associated temples throughout Japan.

Jack walked up to one of the monks at the entrance directing tourist groups assembling at the gate. Dressed in traditional garb usually worn by working monks, the monk took one look at the name on the piece of paper Jack showed him and took him aside. 'How did you come by this name, sir?' he asked in perfect English, scrutinising Jack with interest.

'It's a long story. My friend and I just flew in from New Zealand this morning. The name and this address were given to us by an art dealer in Auckland. Are we in the right place? Does this name mean anything to you?'

'It does. Just give me a moment and we'll go somewhere quiet where we can talk about this.'

Jack looked at Tristan and nodded.

'I knew we were in the right place as soon as we walked in here,' said Tristan.

'How come?'

Tristan shrugged. 'Just a feeling. There's something very special about this place; liquid peace. So many voices …'

'You are not talking about the tourists, are you?'

'Certainly not. These are voices from the past.'

'Whispering angels?' teased Jack.

'No. Some of them are more like snarling dragons and demons.'

'Ah. Let's see what the monk has to tell us. The name certainly seems to mean something to him. You should have seen his face when I showed him the note. He looked rattled.'

The monk returned a few minutes later, ushered them through the crowded entrance and took them to the chou-on-tei, the 'garden of the sound of the tide', a beautiful, secluded Zen garden famous for its *san-zon-seki*, a Buddhist stone arrangement often used as a focal point for meditation.

'That's better,' said the monk. 'Let's have a seat on the bench here.'

'This is magnificent,' said Tristan, his head spinning from an onslaught of voices reaching out from the past.

'And so peaceful,' added Jack.

'The name you just showed me is the name of our abbot before his ordination. That was a long time ago. He took the name Moro after he became abbot. Few know his real name. He was an acclaimed potter before he became a monk. That's why I was so surprised when you showed me the note.'

'According to the New Zealand art dealer I mentioned, the man whose name appears on the piece of paper I showed you bought a painting by a famous New Zealand artist, Charles Goldie, at auction a few years ago. For a lot of money. Over the phone. A portrait to be precise, of Parema Te Pahau, a famous Māori warrior chief who was killed in battle on the Chatham Islands in 1840.'

'Intriguing,' said the monk.

'Would it be possible for us to meet the abbot?' said Jack.

'I'm afraid not. He's very elderly and quite frail. Almost blind. He lives in a monastery close by, and no longer leaves his quarters. He just turned a hundred.'

Jack nodded. 'Is there anyone else we could talk to about the painting?'

'I can talk to the abbot, if you like. He may be frail, but his mind is as sharp and as clear as that of a man half his age. So, what is your interest in this painting? What would you like to know about it and why; provided, of course, that Abbot Tetsudo Moro did in fact acquire it, as you suggest?'

Jack sat back, collecting his thoughts, and for a while contemplated the peaceful garden. Then, speaking softly, he told the monk about the significance of Goldie's painting, what it meant – especially to Tristan and his grandmother – and why finding it was so important. He also told him about Tristan's promise to locate and retrieve the *Mokomokai*, and why the facial tattoo in the painting was the only way to identify the mummified head of his ancestor, should it be possible to find it.

'That's quite a story,' said the monk. 'If I understand you correctly, what you are really after is an image of the painting showing the tattoo, the *moko* as I think you called it, depicted in the portrait?'

'Correct.'

'The abbot will be very interested in this amazing story, and I can assure you, he will be very understanding.'

'I'm glad to hear it, but something puzzles me,' said Jack. 'Why would the abbot of a famous Zen Buddhist temple here in Japan be interested in a painting of a dead Māori chief who was killed in the New Zealand Wars more than one hundred and fifty years ago?'

'Ah. Only Abbot Tetsudo Moro can answer that, but as an accomplished artist himself, he has been very interested in art all his life and has acquired many artworks for the temple over the years. You see, he believes that art is another language; another, often secret way of communicating, especially when esoteric subjects are involved, accessible only to the initiated few. We have an extraordinary art collection here in our temple, dealing with precisely such subjects.'

'And the Goldie portrait is part of this collection?'

'Most likely, yes.'

'Because it has some esoteric value?'

The monk shrugged, but didn't reply.

'I see. So, where to from here?' said Jack.

'I will speak to the abbot about this tonight,' said the monk and stood up.

'Thank you. We are grateful.'

Tristan, who had been staring at the *san-zon-seki*, the Buddhist stone arrangement in the garden, while Jack had been telling his story, stood up as well. 'Before we go, I have a message for the abbot,' he said softly.

'Oh? What message?' asked the monk, surprised.

Tristan pointed to the *san-zon-seki*. 'Actually, it's a message from that stone over there,' he said.

The monk looked puzzled. 'What do you mean?'

'While you two have been talking, I've been listening to the stone's whispers.'

'Oh? And what was it whispering about?'

'Abbot Tetsudo Moro.'

Bemused, the monk looked at Tristan. 'Can you tell us more?' he asked.

'I had a vision. The abbot was lying on his bed facing a window overlooking a walled garden. Above the bed I could see a picture.'

'What kind of picture?' asked the monk, frowning.

'A scroll painting by Hakuin Ekaku.'

'Can you describe it?'

'It's all about a *kōan*, a paradoxical parable.'

'What parable?'

'What is the sound of one hand clapping?'

The monk shook his head, wondering how he could possibly know this. 'How—?' he asked, lost for words.

'I just saw it. The abbot received this picture as a gift on his eighty-fourth birthday, and it has been hanging above his bed ever since.'

'I don't know what to say. This is astonishing!'

'There's more.'

'What do you mean?'

'The following is written on the back of the picture:

"An elderly monk of eighty-four, I welcome in yet one year more

And I owe it all – everything – to the sound of one hand clapping."'

Stunned, the monk looked at Tristan. 'Who *are* you?'

'I am Tristan Te Papatahi, a direct descendant of Parema Te Pahau, who was a *tohunga matakite*, a revered Māori foreteller of the future. I am the last in line and I am turning to Abbot Tetsudo Moro for help—'

'To fulfil a promise?'

'Yes. To help a lost soul enter the afterlife. The sound of one hand clapping …'

The monk nodded. He apparently understood the meaning of the cryptic message. 'Come back here tomorrow just after sunrise before the tourists arrive, and I will bring you Abbot Tetsudo Moro's answer. They call me Ikkyu, by the way.'

'And I am Jack Rogan. Greatly appreciated,' said Jack, making a bow. 'We'll be there.'

'What was all that about?' asked Jack as they were leaving the temple. 'The sound of one hand clapping?'

'I sent the abbot a message.'

'Oh? What kind of message?'

'A Zen message I knew he would understand.'

'*He* may, but I don't.'

'"The sound of one hand clapping" is a famous Zen *kōan*, a puzzle. It's not about solitude or meditating alone, as one might expect. It's a realisation that there is another hand somewhere out there, in need just like yours. This is a Zen lesson to show us that we need each other and must help each other and reach out, because without the other hand, there is no clapping.'

'How do you know all this?'

'The rock told me.'

'Ah …' said Jack, realising Tristan's occult powers were becoming stronger at an astounding rate. The whisper of angels was turning into a chorus of heavenly voices, guiding him through the valley of tears.

Dharma Hall, Kennin-ji Temple, Kyoto: 2 October

Ikkyu was already waiting at the deserted temple gate by the time Jack and Tristan arrived. It was just after sunrise.

'Here we go,' said Jack, enjoying the bracing air of the clear morning heralding a beautiful new day. 'I hope what he has to tell us is in keeping with this stunning morning.'

'It will be, trust me,' said Tristan. 'The sound of one hand clapping is very powerful, remember?'

'Let's hope that the missing hand in the parable is reaching out to help us.'

'Good morning, gentlemen,' said Ikkyu as he opened the gate. 'I hope you had a restful night? Please follow me.'

'Yes, we did, thank you. Where are we going?' asked Jack, watching Ikkyu carefully, but the monk's inscrutable facial expression gave nothing away.

'The Dharma Hall. I want to show you something. The Dharma Hall is one of the most popular attractions here. You'll see why in a moment. And besides, it's a very pertinent place for what I have to say.'

'Isn't that where senior monks used to preach?' said Jack, his curiosity aroused.

'Correct. It's a lecture hall, a place of learning, and ours here is one of the most spectacular in Kyoto. It was built in 1765. Early morning before the tourists arrive is the best time to see it. Come.'

As soon as Tristan entered the Hatto, as the Dharma Hall was called, his eyes went straight to the ceiling, dominated by a stunning painting. 'Breathtaking,' he said and pointed to the ceiling.

'Isn't it?' said Ikkyu. '*Twin Dragons* by Koizumi Junsaku. It's the size of a hundred and eight tatami mats, roughly eleven by sixteen metres. It commemorates the eight hundredth anniversary of the temple and was installed here in 2002, but it wasn't painted here.'

'Oh? How come?' asked Jack.

'The artist, a famous painter and potter, was almost eighty at the time he painted this. It took him two years to complete and was painted in a gym of a school in Hokkaido. Ink on traditional Japanese paper. Very labour intensive, especially for an artist of advanced years.'

'The dragons are obviously significant – symbolically, I mean,' said Jack.

'Yes, they are. The dragon is a symbol of enlightenment, transformation and wisdom in Buddhist teaching, and a revered protector of *dharma*, which in Buddhism means cosmic law and order. The Dharma Rain of Buddhist teaching brings new life and enlightenment to all, and offers liberation from suffering.'

'I hope it can do all that for us,' said Tristan, steering the conversation back to what was obviously on everyone's mind.

The monk looked up at the ceiling and pointed to one of the dragons staring down at him from above. 'Abbot Tetsudo Moro has carefully considered your request, and his response is in accord with the Dharma Rain,' he said. 'Yes, the Goldie painting was acquired by him and is in our collection here at the temple.'

The monk turned towards Tristan. 'The abbot recognises in you a kindred spirit searching for enlightenment. Your promise to find your ancestor's head and facilitate his entry into the afterlife is a manifestation of important virtues like kindness, generosity and compassion. From now on, you will no longer walk alone and hear the sound of one hand clapping, because the abbot has answered your call for help.'

Relieved, Jack took a deep breath and also looked up at the dragons.

The monk pulled his iPhone out of his pocket. 'I have here several images of Parema Te Pahau's portrait I can send you.'

Visibly moved, Tristan nodded. 'Please convey my heartfelt thanks to the abbot for his help and generosity of spirit. Now that I'm no longer alone, I will continue my search with renewed vigour.'

Ikkyu nodded. 'Abbot Tetsudo Moro has one request,' he added quietly.

'What kind of request?' asked Tristan.

'To be kept informed about your search, wherever it may take you. You can do that by calling me. I see the abbot almost every day.'

'We'll gladly do that. If Parema Te Pahau's head is still somewhere out there, looking for peace, I will find it and return it to where it belongs,' said Tristan. 'That, I have promised.'

Jack and Tristan caught the *shinkansen* back to Osaka airport later that day. Their flight was due to leave in the evening, but Jack had changed the itinerary. He found the pictures Ikkyu had sent him on his iPhone and showed them again to Tristan sitting next to him.

'What do you think?' he said.

'Stunning portrait. Goldie has done an outstanding job recreating the face, bearing in mind that the subject had been dead for many years by the time he painted this, and he was using the *Mokomokai* as his inspiration, I suppose. It shows every detail of the *moko*.'

'That's what he's famous for.'

'I can see why. This should be more than enough to identify the head; if we manage to find it, that is. That's the million-dollar question here, right?'

'It is, and you will be pleased to hear that I've already prepared the next step we should take.'

'No doubt about you, Jack. Tell me.'

'Well, who do we know in the art world who could help us in our search, especially in the UK, where we must start? Someone who is not only well connected but can open doors for us that you and I wouldn't even know existed—'

'Isis, of course. Who else?'

'Correct. That's why I changed our flight.'

'You did?'

'We're catching a flight to London, not Venice. Boris will pick us up at Heathrow and take us to the Time Machine Studios. Isis is waiting, chomping at the bit to become part of the search.'

'You spoke to her already?'

'I did.'

'You're keen, Jack.'

'No point in wasting time.'

'I agree.'

'If Parema Te Pahau's head is still around, we'll find it,' said Jack.

'You bet.'

Jack opened his duffel bag, took out his notebook and opened it. 'Don't forget, the head became part of the Robley collection of thirty-five *Mokomokai*; so much, we know. According to your grandmother, the collection was repatriated in 2014 from the American Museum of Natural History in New York—'

'As part of the Karanga Aotearoa Repatriation Programme,' said Tristan.

'Correct. And ended up in the Te Papa Museum in Wellington. But unfortunately, Parema Te Pahau's head wasn't among the *Mokomokai* because Robley had kept five of the best heads for himself at the time he sold his collection to the Americans. That was in 1908, I believe. It is reasonable to assume the head we're looking for was one of those he retained.'

'Well then, that's our starting point, yes?' said Tristan.

Jack closed his notebook. 'It is. In short, what happened to the five *Mokomokai* that Robley kept for himself? That's what we have to find out. Something so unique doesn't just disappear. I already told Isis all about this, and she came up with some ideas ...'

'*Seriously?* What kind of ideas?' asked Tristan.

'She didn't say. That's why we are going to London. To find out.'

'Jack the old newshound at work?' joked Tristan. 'Following the trail of another hot story?'

Jack shrugged and slipped his notebook into the duffel bag.

Tristan pointed out of the window. 'Look, we're almost there. Ready to face the rush for the doors?'

'I am.'

'Don't lose your phone, whatever you do!'

'I've already sent the images to Isis,' said Jack.

'Smart move. Let's go!'

Time Machine Studios, London: 3 October

Boris, Isis's bodyguard-cum-chauffeur, greeted Jack and Tristan with his customary, chest-crushing bear hug – a sign of genuine affection – and drove them straight from Heathrow to the Time Machine Studios in central London.

'How is she?' asked Jack, who hadn't seen Isis for a few months.

'A little preoccupied lately,' said Boris.

'Oh? Do you know why?'

'Not for me to say.'

'Come on, we've been around Isis for a long time now, you and I. Not just friends; you and Lola are family.'

'Perhaps the closest family Isis has,' interjected Tristan.

Boris shrugged, his massive former-wrestling-champion frame occupying not only the driver's seat but also part of the passenger seat next to it as well. 'That's why.'

'That's why what?' said Jack.

'It's not for me to say.'

Jack glanced at Tristan sitting next to him in the back of the old Bentley and saw the concerned look on his face. *He knows something's wrong,* thought Jack.

'We'll ask Lola,' said Tristan.

'You do that,' said Boris. 'Better that way.'

Lola, Isis's PA, confidante and pilot, was waiting for them in the underground garage.

'Boris said that Isis has seemed somewhat preoccupied lately,' said Jack as they were waiting for the private lift to take them up to the penthouse. Jack had noticed that Lola seemed uncharacteristically subdued. 'Anything in that?'

'She's seen Sir Humphrey several times lately and it wasn't for a game of chess. She's due for a check-up with Professor Greenberg in Boston shortly. We're flying over.'

'A little bedside espionage like last time? Routine, surely? She's seen him regularly since the operation.'

In 2011, Isis had spectacularly collapsed on stage during a concert in Mexico City. Caused by an insidious brain tumour, thought to be inoperable, Isis had been referred to Professor Greenberg who, against all odds, had managed to operate and save her life.

Instead of replying, Lola kept pressing the lift button.

'Come on, Lola, is there something we should know?' Jack pushed.

'Your phone call from Kyoto came at a good time,' said Lola, ignoring the question. 'Isis has barely slept or left her study since.'

'Why?'

'She wanted to make some progress before you arrived. Surprise you—'

'About the missing head?' said Tristan.

'We've done a lot of research together. I've learned heaps about *Mokomokai*, Musket Wars, facial tattoos, the bizarre Robley collection of mummified Māori heads, and a lot more.'

'And has she? Made progress, I mean?' said Jack.

'I'll let her tell you about that. Ah, here's the lift at last. I don't know what took so long,' said Lola. As the lift doors opened, she put her hand on Tristan's arm. 'Your tattoo looks incredible. Isis will love it.'

'You think so?'

'Absolutely. You know what she's like.'

'We sure do. Always on the lookout for the outrageous and exotic,' said Jack.

'You know, don't you?' said Lola softly as the lift reached the penthouse. She was obviously referring to Isis.

'Yes,' replied Tristan.

'Care to tell me?' said Jack.

Tristan shook his head and followed Lola out of the lift.

Isis was sitting at her desk in her study on the top floor. Dressed in simple active wear instead of her usual flamboyant designer clothes, her hair a little dishevelled and with bags under her eyes, she looked like someone who hadn't slept after a rough night on the booze, rather than the billionaire rockstar fashion icon who never set foot outside her bedroom without impeccable makeup and dressed to kill, whatever the occasion.

'Good flight?' she said, her voice sounding hoarse, and embraced Jack and Tristan, the hugs a little hesitant.

'Yes, thank you,' said Jack, unable to hide the concern in his voice.

Isis pointed to Tristan's face. 'Wow! Look at you,' she said. 'I want one of these.'

'You can't,' said Tristan, smiling.

'Why not?'

'You aren't Māori.'

'What if I give a concert in New Zealand?'

'No chance.'

'Even if I help you find your ancestor's head?' said Isis, a little of the old sparkle in her eyes.

'You know something?' said Tristan.

'Perhaps. Now let's have some champagne,' said Isis. 'Lola, please?'

'Are you sure? Remember what Sir Humphrey said …'

'Absolutely. I haven't seen these guys in months.'

'As you wish,' said Lola and left the room.

Jack walked over to Isis, standing by the window, and put his arm around her shoulders. 'What's wrong?' he said softly.

'It's back.'

'What is?'

Jack could feel Isis beginning to tremble. 'The tumour,' she whispered.

'How do you know?'

'Tests.'

'How serious?'

'We won't know until Greenberg has a look. We're flying over—'

'It's nothing,' interjected Tristan, looking at the Tower Bridge lit up in the distance.

Both Jack and Isis turned around, surprised.

'How can you say that?' asked Isis.

'Because I know.'

'Now, hold on, mate,' said Jack. 'This is *serious*.'

'I know.'

'How can you possibly—?'

'Her body told me. Just now when she gave me a hug.'

Jack looked at Isis and shrugged.

'Enough of that!' said Isis as Lola walked in carrying an ice bucket with a bottle of champagne, and four crystal flutes. 'Let's have a drink.'

'Good idea,' said Jack, welcoming the change of subject.

'Now, tell me all about this fascinating trip of yours,' said Isis, sipping her champagne.

'It all began with a phone call from New Zealand,' said Jack.

'When was that?' asked Isis.

'About two weeks ago. Tristan's uncle, the Bone Scraper, was dying in Auckland, and wanted to see Tristan,' said Jack.

'How interesting. *Bone Scraper?* Funny name,' said Lola.

'He was the leader of a notorious Māori gang in Auckland.'

'He was more than that,' said Tristan. 'My whole world changed that day.'

'In what way?' said Isis.

'The moment my uncle died, I felt something change inside me,' said Tristan, looking dreamily out of the window. 'It was as if something had passed from him to me, like a third eye that allowed me to see things in different ways. I know this may sound weird and make no sense, but I don't know how else to express it. Jack's much better with words than I—'

'Don't worry, you're doing fine,' interrupted Isis, hanging on Tristan's every word, like a drowning man clutching a lifeline. 'Please, go on.'

Encouraged, Tristan gave a detailed account of the events following the Bone Scraper's death in Auckland, right up to the parting conversation with the monk in the Dharma Hall in the Kennin-ji Temple in Kyoto.

'No doubt about you two,' said Isis. 'Excitement and adventure seem to follow you every step of the way.'

'Except this time, it's very personal. I feel like my whole existence, my very reason for being, are hanging in the balance,' said Tristan, looking suddenly drained and tired.

'As you can see, this trip has taken a lot out of him,' said Jack, stepping in. 'Things will look very different in the morning.'

'I'm sure you're right. Would you mind very much if I were to turn in?' said Tristan, slowly tracing his *moko* with the tips of his fingers.

'Not at all,' said Isis. 'Lola will show you to your room.'

'He has changed,' said Isis, after Tristan and Lola had left.

Jack nodded. 'You're right. I've never seen him like this. We both know he's an extraordinary young man, with powers and insights that are difficult to comprehend at times, but what seems to be happening to him right now is in a league of its own. I'm in awe of him. His powers seem to be growing stronger by the day, especially since the Bone Scraper died and he met his grandmother. Even his voice seems to be changing.'

'His *grandmother*? He didn't mention her. I wonder why?'

'Not sure, but she seems to think that Tristan has the psychic gift that has been passed down in her family from generation to generation. His mother had it, only his is much stronger. This search for the missing head is part of it because Parema Te Pahau, the famous ancestor, could see into the future.'

'And what do you make of all this?' asked Isis.

'I agree. Something strange is going on here, that's for sure. I hate the term supernatural, but it's certainly spiritual and *real*. I just can't explain it.'

'Do you think there could be something in what Tristan just said? About my condition, I mean?'

Jack took his time before replying because he realised what this could mean to Isis. Especially in her state.

'He wouldn't have said it unless he *believed* it to be true,' said Jack, choosing his words carefully.

'Thanks, Jack. I can't tell you what this means to me. As you know, I have been interested in esoteric subjects for years, especially as far as my music is concerned. It all comes down to whether you believe in the spirit world. Tristan obviously does, and so do I. The Rosicrucians – Paracelsus in particular – and the Freemasons, all played an important part in the lives of such greats as Mozart and Beethoven. It has often been said Mozart must have been taking dictation from God when he composed his sublime music. Perhaps he entered a different consciousness when he composed, and crossed over into the spirit world? Who knows?'

'What about you? What happens when you compose? You told me that you find inspiration in classical music,' said Jack, pleased to see Isis's mood had significantly improved. 'Do you enter into a different consciousness?'

'Good question. I have never told you this, but before I start composing, I listen to Beethoven's *Appassionata*, his Piano Sonata No. 23, one of his most technically challenging works. Pure genius.'

'Why?'

'To me, it's a trigger. When I listen to this piece of music, my mind begins to wander and a sense of calmness descends.'

'Then what?'

'Creative ideas appear and float into my consciousness. I have no idea where they come from, but they are real, beautiful, unique.'

'And then?'

'I begin to work like a man – no, a woman – possessed, trying to capture these ideas before they retreat like morning fog among the trees and are lost forever. It's all about creativity and inspiration.'

'Dictation from God?' teased Jack.

'Not quite. I'm not Amadeus.'

'You are a rock star admired by millions.'

'*Resurrection*, one of my greatest hits, isn't the *Appassionata*—'

'You're too modest.'

'You think so?'

Jack smiled. Isis was quickly returning to her old self, and it seemed to have been caused by one sentence Tristan had uttered earlier. That in itself was remarkable, thought Jack.

'Now, why don't you tell me what you've found out so far?' said Jack, changing direction.

'About that missing head? Fascinating stuff. As you said on the phone, the Robley collection is our starting point. Our best chance of finding Parema Te Pahau's mummified head, traded for muskets during a colonial war in New Zealand. Lola and I did some digging.'

'Oh? Any luck?'

'Judge for yourself. We came up with a possible lead: William Ockleford Oldman.'

'Who on earth is William—?'

'Ockleford Oldman. He was a British collector who purchased collections from various sources, including private collectors like Robley. His main interest was – wait for it – Oceania.'

'Interesting …'

'It's more than that, as you'll see in a moment.'

Jack reached for his glass of champagne and took a sip. 'Can't wait,' he said.

'Oldman bought some of Robley's remaining collection after Robley sold the *Mokomokai* to the American Museum of Natural History in 1908. Robley kept the five best heads for himself, remember?'

'Correct.'

'I think I know what happened to them.'

'*You do*?' said Jack and almost spilled his champagne.

'What Lola and I found is this …' Isis stood up, walked over to her desk and held up a sheet of paper.

'What's that?'

'A copy of an artefacts list Oldman used to send to his contacts on a monthly basis. A bit like a catalogue illustrated with photographs like this one here, which also contains provenance of the items on offer. This was after 1913. He no longer conducted auctions by then, but concentrated on private sales to museums and collectors. This was a lucrative business, and today many museums around the world have pieces in their collections acquired from Oldman.'

'And this is relevant because?'

Isis walked over to Jack and handed him the piece of paper. 'Because of this. Here, judge for yourself.'

Momentarily speechless, Jack stared at the page in his hand. On top of the page was a faded black-and-white photograph showing five of what looked like tattooed heads hanging on a wall. The image was too blurred and grainy to be able to discern individual features. The caption below the photograph stated:

'Five Māori Mokomokai *in excellent condition acquired from the private collection of Major General Horatio Gordon Robley, who spent many years in New Zealand, and built up a large collection of* Mokomokai. *The collection was sold to the American Museum of Natural History in 1908. These five tattooed Māori heads were retained by Robley, as they represented the finest pieces in that collection, and are now offered for sale for the first time.'*

'I don't know what to say,' said Jack. 'This is amazing.'

'Lola found it on the Net.'

'Do we know who bought the heads?'

'Unfortunately, no. Not *yet.'*

'What do you mean?'

'I think to trace the buyer here, especially after such a long time, we need a specialist.'

'A *specialist?* What kind of specialist?' asked Jack.

'Someone who specialises in authenticating artworks and curios by way of establishing provenance, and other distinguishing features.'

'And such experts exist?'

'Absolutely, and I happen to know two of the best in the business,' said Isis.

'You do? You're full of surprises. Who?'

'Have you heard of *Real or Fake?* A TV show here in the UK? It was broadcast some time ago. Very popular.'

'Can't say I have.'

'It was run by a husband-and-wife team, Cybil and Richard Craigieburn. Art historians. They had an art gallery in Mayfair for years. They are quite elderly now, but still active. They take on private assignments, authenticating artworks. I've used them on several occasions.'

'Like we did with Monet's *Little Sparrow in the Garden* in Switzerland? Exposing the Fuchs forgery?'

'The Emil Fuchs affair. Wasn't that something? *The Forgotten Painting*. Exactly. And Cybil and Richard are just like Jacques Moreau, the Monet expert, whose word was final when it came to authentication.'

'Let's hope they are as good as Moreau was.'

'They are. Trust me.'

Isis walked over to an easel with a painting on the frame and turned it around to face Jack. 'Here it is. The original Monet: *Little Sparrow in the Garden*. And over there by the bookcase is the forgery by David Herzl, the Postmaster of Treblinka, which caused such a stir at the time. As you know, Fuchs left it to me.'

'You have a part of history in here that has touched us all.'

'And you keep telling me that we're only temporary custodians of other men's genius.'

'Touché.'

'Be that as it may, this here is part of my life, and you and Tristan are part of it. We are all interconnected and that's what counts for the moment.'

'So, what was this *Real or Fake?* show all about?'

'People used to bring artworks and curios to the live show, paintings mainly, to find out if they were authentic or not. Once selected, the items became part of the show, and Cybil and Richard went to work like proper art detectives. Their methods and results were remarkable. The climax of the show, often several weeks later, was a great reveal, usually involving experts in the field, who appeared on the show to tell the anxious owner and the curious audience if the piece was a fake, or the real thing. The latter was usually worth a small fortune. Exciting stuff like that.'

'I think I can see where this is heading,' said Jack.

'I'm sure you can. We're having afternoon tea with Cybil and Richard at Claridge's tomorrow. They love Claridge's and so do I. I meet them there often.'

Jack shook his head, amazed.

Smiling for the first time that evening, Isis reached for the champagne bottle. 'A little more?' she said and held up the bottle. 'Hopefully, we'll be able to share many more bottles like this in the future.'

'Count me in,' said Jack and held up his empty glass.

Afternoon tea at Claridge's, Mayfair, London: 4 October

'Where is she?' asked Jack impatiently. They had been waiting in the lounge for Isis for more than an hour.

'She hasn't come out of her room all morning. Slept in. Even had breakfast in bed, which is unusual,' said Lola. 'The maid took it in.'

Tristan looked at his watch. 'If we want to make it to Claridge's by three, we have to leave now. Do you want to go upstairs and see what's going on?'

'No need. Here she comes now,' said Lola. 'Look.'

Isis knew how to make an entrance. She stopped at the top of the stairs and adjusted her hair before slowly descending. This was a ritual well known to all. Dressed in a stunning, Prussian-blue, figure-hugging pantsuit by Olivier Rousteing, creative director of Balmain, and a pair of Tiffany diamond earrings fit for a tsarina, she looked like a fashion model who had just stepped off the runway at Paris Fashion Week. Dramatic, almost theatrical makeup and carefully coiffured hair completed the look.

Aware everyone was watching her, Isis stopped halfway down the stairs and looked down into the lounge. 'What do you think, guys? A little over the top for afternoon tea at Claridge's?'

'Not at all,' said Jack, smiling. 'You look fabulous.' *Must've taken her hours to get ready*, he thought, resisting the urge to clap.

'You really think so? A few pounds off the hips would have helped.'

Lola rolled her eyes and looked at Tristan, who tried hard not to laugh.

'Never mind. It is what it is, and I'm going to have some of the sandwiches *and* the sweets, regardless. Growing old is such a bitch and dieting such a bore, don't you think so, Lola?'

'If you say so,' said Lola, who had heard it all before, but was delighted to see Isis back to her old self again.

'Are you ready? Let's go!' said Isis, balancing carefully on insanely high heels and heading for the lift.

The doorman walked up to the Bentley as it pulled up in front of the imposing entrance of Claridge's, one of London's most famous hotels, and opened the back door.

'Wonderful to see you, again, Ma'am,' he said and helped Isis get out of the car. 'Are you here for afternoon tea?'

'Yes. I have reserved a table in the Library Room.'

'Excellent choice.'

Isis linked arms with Jack and swept into the elegant foyer, well aware she was turning heads. For an attention seeker like Isis, being noticed was ego-oxygen she couldn't live without.

'I love the flowers and the décor, don't you?' she said, following the Maître d' into the Library Room.

'Stunning.'

'Did you know that in 1945, Churchill declared suite 212 Yugoslavian territory so that Crown Prince Alexander II could be born in his own country?'

'You don't say,' said Jack.

'In the 1950s, Claridge's was all the rage with the Hollywood stars, many of whom made this place their London residence. Katherine Hepburn, Cary Grant, Yul Brynner, and Bing Crosby virtually lived here. *Can you imagine?* How I would have loved to have been part of that!'

'I can imagine,' mumbled Jack.

'All we have now is social media, influencers and the internet. What a bore! Thank God for places like this. Ah, there they are. *Mokomokai* time! Come, let me introduce you.'

The Craigieburns turned out to be excellent company. Honed by years of standing in front of the camera working with a live audience, their polished social skills were witty and entertaining. Despite their advanced years, they knew how to keep the conversation going and make everyone at the table feel at ease.

The splendid afternoon tea, showcasing Claridge's signature tasty morsels, both sweet and savoury, served on traditional Bernardaud china platters with jade and blue chevrons, added a touch of elegance and class that had given Claridge's an enviable reputation that even the Royal Family had found irresistible over the years. Prince Albert had started it all in the 1890s, and the Queen Mother had been a frequent visitor over the years, enjoying her famous gin and Dubonnet before lunch.

Cybil, a flamboyant dresser like Isis, took an instant shine to Jack and began to flirt with him in subtle ways. She reminded him of his friend Mademoiselle Darrieux and her antics, but in an endearingly entertaining way.

'Did you know that the Queen Mother used to lunch here often?' said Cybil.

'I can understand why. It's only a short distance from Buckingham Palace,' said Jack.

'That may have been part of it. Her lunches were as legendary as her hats. To this very day, her favourite table in the restaurant is still decorated with sweet peas, in her memory.'

'I wouldn't mind being remembered in that way,' said Isis. 'One day perhaps, but not yet—'

'When the sailing ships from heaven come calling?' said Lola, smiling.

Isis waved dismissively. 'Something like that.'

Once the table had been cleared, with only the teacups remaining, the conversation turned to the subject that had brought them all together.

'Jack, why don't you tell us about your New Zealand trip?' said Isis.

Jack had been expecting this and was ready. The storyteller was in his element. He put his notebook on the table in front of him and gave a detailed account not only of the recent trip, but also of certain events leading up to it, to put the fascinating subject matter into proper context.

'And then we have this,' he said and placed on the table an enlarged image of the Goldie portrait he had obtained from the monk Ikkyu in Kyoto.

'Is this—?' asked Richard.

'It is,' said Tristan. 'This is Parema Te Pahau, a famous Māori warrior chief who was killed in battle on the Chatham Islands in 1840.'

'Needless to say, this is most helpful. At least we know what he looked like. The tattoos in particular will help us identify the *Mokomokai* we are looking for,' said Richard.

'There is more,' said Jack, sounding like a magician introducing his next trick, and put the Oldman catalogue page with the photo of the five Māori heads on the table next to the Goldie portrait image. 'Lola found this on the Net.'

Richard picked up the page and studied it carefully. 'This is excellent – and fortuitous,' he said. 'Oldman was very active in the art world and very thorough. He kept meticulous records. We have traced and authenticated numerous pieces over the years, using those records.'

Richard handed the page to his wife and looked at Tristan sitting opposite. 'Are you suggesting that one of these five heads is the head we are looking for?'

'Most likely, yes. Pity the image is so blurred. Otherwise ...'

'Never mind,' said Cybil. 'It's enough for a good start. This is more than we had to go by on many occasions, don't you think, Richard?'

'Absolutely.'

'I prepared a small dossier last night summarising what we've found out so far,' said Jack. 'I can send it to you, if you like.'

'Please do. That would be most helpful,' said Richard. 'We're off to a good start, don't you think so, Cybil?'

'Definitely.'

'So, where to from here?' said Jack.

'Cybil and I will get down to work straight away. If we have any questions, we'll get in touch.'

'And please make me the contact point in this,' interjected Isis, obviously keen to remain involved.

'Will do,' said Richard.

Isis signalled to the waiter walking past. 'This calls for champagne, don't you think?'

'Definitely,' said Cybil, a sparkle in her eyes. 'Claridge's never disappoints, and neither do you.'

On the way to Paris: 13 October

Jack was enjoying a nightcap in his study on the ground floor of his new home – Palazzo Alberti on the Grand Canal – when his mobile rang. It was well past midnight. He pushed aside the renovation plans he had been studying and answered the phone. It was Isis.

'I just had a call from Richard Craigieburn,' she said, sounding excited. It had been just over a week since their meeting at Claridge's.

'Any news?'

'Looks that way.' Isis paused, to let the tension grow.

'Well, are you going to tell me, or just kill me slowly with suspense?'

'Nothing like it. Actually, he told me very little, except for this ...'

'Well?'

'They managed to trace the five *Mokomokai* that Oldman bought from Robley. The Oldman records made this possible. Apparently, four heads went to museums in Europe and are accounted for—'

'And?'

'That leaves one.'

'Obviously.'

'The fifth head was bought by a Paris socialite, a notorious lady with a colourful background and quite a reputation ...'

'What kind of reputation? Do we know more?' asked Jack.

'We do. She had an interest in the occult and – listen to this – she was reputed to be some kind of *medium*.'

'And is this helpful? Do we know more about the head she bought? Could it be the one we're looking for?'

'Yes.'

'What makes you say that?'

'Process of elimination. Apparently, Richard was able to obtain images of the four heads that ended up in museums. He has excellent contacts. None of them look like the head we are looking for. The *moko* are different.'

'That's helpful.'

93

'It is.'

'Have Richard and Cybil been able to find out more about this socialite dabbling in the occult?'

'Investigations are continuing, that's all I know. But there must be more.'

'What makes you say that?'

'Richard wants to meet us, urgently.'

'Oh? That's interesting. Where?'

'In Paris.'

'When?'

'As soon as possible.'

'How about tomorrow? Can you get there?' said Jack.

'Just try to stop me. What about you?'

'I'll work something out.'

'I'll let him know. Where shall we meet?'

'I know just the place,' said Jack.

'Tell me.'

'The Craigieburns loved Claridge's and so do you, right?'

'Absolutely, it's one of my favourite hotels in London.'

'Then you will like the place I have in mind.'

'What place?' asked Isis.

'How about lunch at La Closerie des Lilas?' said Jack.

'Excellent suggestion. I know it well. Good choice. You obviously know the restaurant?'

'I had an unforgettable experience there with Mademoiselle Darrieux a few years ago.'

'All experiences with her are unforgettable.'

'How right you are. Shall we say one? Hopefully, I'll be able to get there in time. Should be able to, if I get an early flight.'

'I'll let them know. Do you want us to pick you up?' said Isis.

'What do you mean?'

'I have a plane, remember? And Lola has been complaining that we aren't going anywhere. She's been itching to fly. The next trip is to Boston for a check-up. Not very exciting. That isn't for a couple of weeks.'

'Are you serious? You'll fly all the way from London to Venice just to pick us up, and then on to Paris for lunch?'

'Why not? I'm due for some excitement, Jack, and you, my friend, are my best bet in that department. And besides, we have friends at Marco Polo Airport, remember? We just slip in, you and Tristan get on board, and on we go.'

'You're on,' said Jack, laughing. 'Hitching a ride on the *Mokomokai Express*!'

'I like that. I'll let you know the time.'

'Thanks, Isis. Tristan will be over the moon.'

'It's all settled then. *What to wear…?* La Closerie des Lilas is such a posh place.'

'I'm sure you'll come up with something,' said Jack, laughing, 'to dazzle the lunch set.'

'Easy for you, my friend. You're a famous writer. You just turn up in jeans and a bomber jacket and everyone thinks you look fabulous. Not that easy for me.'

'You're the head-turner, not me.'

'You think so?'

'Absolutely.'

'Paris … I'll wear something French. You know what the French are like. They think they own fashion and everyone else is just a pedestrian upstart with no class.'

'Sounds like a great idea. See you tomorrow at the airport.'

Pegasus landed just after seven am the next day at Venice Marco Polo Airport and taxied to the designated spot reserved for private jets. Jack and Tristan were asked to wait in the transit lounge.

'What now?' asked Tristan.

'Wait and see,' said Jack, who had seen it all before. 'Look over there.' Jack pointed to one of the double doors.

'What am I looking at?'

'Isis fans waiting for their idol. You know how popular she is in Italy.'

'You're joking. They look like airport staff.'

'Exactly. That's what they are. Cleaners, baggage handlers, security guards. And there's a good reason for this. Watch ... Ah, here she comes now.'

The doors leading to the tarmac opened and Isis swept into the room. Looking glamorous as always, she was waving and blowing kisses in all directions. The excited crowd surged forward and Isis began to sign T-shirts, lunchboxes, pieces of paper, even a baby held up by a starry-eyed mother who was obviously a fan.

'Ah, there you are, guys. We'll leave in a moment. Just give me a second,' said Isis, clearly enjoying herself.

'Just look at her. Back to her old self, wouldn't you say?' said Jack.

'Basking in adulation, you mean?'

'Something like that. Better than moping around?'

'Definitely. So, what's next?'

'This is the deal: the airport officials cut through all the red tape involved in landing here just to pick up passengers. Normally, that would take hours, but not today. In return, Isis comes in here and signs autographs for the staff. It's a simple trade. Everybody wins. After all, this is Venice. As you well know, trade runs in the blood of the locals here. They've done it for centuries.'

Tristan shook his head. 'You're kidding.'

'Not at all. The reason we'll get going in a minute and make it to lunch in Paris on time is this: a celebrity autograph stopover. Simple.'

'Amazing.'

'Look, she's ready to go. Come on!'

Lunch at La Closerie des Lilas, Paris: 14 October

After an early whirlwind flight from London to Venice to collect Jack and Tristan, and then on to Paris for the lunch date with the Craigieburns, the intrepid travellers made it just on time to La Closerie des Lilas.

Asking Mademoiselle Darrieux, who was a regular, to make a reservation had been a good move, as the place was fully booked, which of course Isis enjoyed, as her carefully timed entrance and slow walk to the coveted table in the middle of the room had its desired effect: admiring looks following her every move, and turning heads with much finger pointing and discreet chatter about her stunning outfit by a leading French designer, which had cost a small fortune.

The Craigieburns had already arrived and were waiting with a welcome bottle of champagne on ice.

'I'm parched,' said Isis as she took a seat next to Richard Craigieburn, in full view of the crowded room. 'We've been on the go since well before dawn. Ghastly! Just look at me. I'm a wreck! The London traffic was diabolical, and coming here from the airport wasn't much better. The French authorities can be so annoying.'

'You mean no motorcycle escort?' teased Lola.

'But we made it – just,' said Isis, ignoring the remark. 'Cheers!'

'You guys do get around,' said Cybil, basking in the admiring glances coming her way from all directions. After all, La Closerie des Lilas was one of *the* Paris society places where one came not necessarily to have lunch, but to be seen.

'Having your own plane helps,' said Jack. 'I don't think Tristan and I would have made it here today any other way.'

'You're here; that's all that matters. Curious?' asked Richard.

'What do you think?' said Isis, holding up her empty glass, which a passing waiter filled immediately.

'You won't be disappointed,' said Cybil. 'Richard, why don't you tell them what we've found out so far?'

'Let's order first. I'm starving,' said Jack, reaching for the menu.

'You're always starving, Jack,' said Lola. 'You're not only an incorrigible rascal, but a bottomless larrikin-pit when it comes to food!'

'I've never been called that before. A bit harsh, don't you think, Tristan?'

'Hm. Some truth in all that.'

'Thanks, mate.'

'The only difference between you and Isis is that she is starving out of choice, aren't you, my dear?' continued Lola, undeterred.

'Not today!' said Isis cheerfully as she reached for the menu.

'What about those extra pounds?' teased Lola.

'Get lost! I'm having escargot and sole meunière. And perhaps even a chocolate soufflé. *Voilà!*'

After the waiter had taken the orders, Richard sat back and looked around the table, obviously enjoying being the centre of attention. Celebrity clients like Isis, with charismatic friends, were rare at his stage in life, and intriguing assignments like the one being discussed, rarer still.

Richard reached for his briefcase, took out a manila folder and placed it ceremoniously on the table in front of him. 'As I told you during our meeting at Claridge's, having Oldfield involved was fortuitous. His records have been most helpful.'

Jack opened his notebook and looked expectantly at Richard. 'In what way?' he asked.

'We've been able to trace all five *Mokomokai* that Oldfield acquired from Robley—'

'I told them about that already,' interjected Isis.

Richard nodded and opened the folder in front of him. 'We have identified the four heads in museums. We actually know where they are. Here are photographs.'

Richard handed the photos around for all to see. 'None of these come even close to the Goldie painting. The *moko* are very different.'

'Agreed,' said Tristan.

'That leaves us with the fifth head. Why don't you take it from here, Cybil? After all, you were the one who found the lead that gave us that breakthrough.'

'All right,' said Cybil, her face flushed with excitement. She riffled through the folder on the table, took out a sepia photograph and held it up. 'It's all about this lady here. Madame Lumière. An incredible character.'

Tristan pointed to the photograph. 'In what way?' he asked.

'The lead in question came from a totally unexpected quarter: the occult. A short, almost insignificant entry in Oldman's auction records mentioned a famous name: Does anyone know who Gérard Encausse was?' asked Cybil, looking around the table, but not expecting a reply.

'He was a French physician, hypnotist and writer, who was heavily involved in occultism. Late nineteenth-century. Very influential,' said Jack.

'He's better known as Papus,' said Tristan. 'He was particularly interested in the cabbala, magic, and the tarot.'

Surprised, Cybil looked at Tristan. 'How on earth do you know this?'

Jack turned to Cybil. 'He can hear the whisper of—'

'*Stop it!*' said Isis. 'How do you know this, Tristan?'

'I was in a coma for years in my early teens after a serious accident. I wasn't expected to live. My late mother, who as you know was a gifted psychic, visited me often in the private clinic where I was on life support. She spoke for hours about the occult and influential writers like Paracelsus, Plato, Robert Fludd, the Rosicrucians, Freemasons and, of course, Papus. She thought I couldn't hear her, but I heard every word, and can still remember everything she said.'

'Astounding,' said Richard, shaking his head.

'The entry in Oldfield's auction records I mentioned indicates that the remaining *Mokomokai* from the Robley connection was purchased by none other than Gérard Encausse. That was in 1905,' continued Cybil.

'Do we know why he bought it, and what he did with it?' asked Jack.

'Obviously, there must have been some occult connection,' said Richard. 'Because Papus was such a well-known and influential figure in French society, there's a lot of material about him and his activities in various archives. He was a member of the Hermetic Brotherhood of Light and the Hermetic Order of the Golden Dawn. So, we began to dig deeper—'

'And then, we found gold,' said Cybil.

'What kind of gold?' asked Jack.

'A specific reference about a tattooed human head with spiritual powers.'

'Seriously? *Where?*' said Isis.

Cybil held up a piece of paper like a trophy. 'In a St Petersburg newspaper article, of all places.'

'You're kidding!' said Jack.

'Papus had close connections to Russia, all the way up to the Imperial family. He visited Russia several times in his capacity as physician and occult consultant to none other than Tsar Nicholas II and Empress Alexandra. Both were very interested in the occult, as was Russian high society at the time. Séances were all the rage.'

Cybil put on her reading glasses and looked at the article.

'And that's where this newspaper article comes into play. Papus visited St Petersburg in 1901, 1905 and 1906,' she said. 'The article claims that Papus was the tsar's mediumistic spiritual adviser, and had a lot of influence on the tsar and the tsarina. Séances at the Winter Palace are specifically mentioned, and so is a human head that was used by Papus as a medium to make contact with the spirit world. It's all in here.'

'Incredible,' said Isis. 'Do you think that this head could—?'

'I understand your question, but there's more. The article goes on to say that during his 1906 visit, Papus made contact with the spirit of Alexander III, the tsar's father, during a séance at the Winter Palace, using – wait for it – a tattooed human "talking" head. Apparently, during the séance, the tsar's father foretold his son's downfall and the murder of his family at the hands of the Bolsheviks,' said Cybil.

'Assuming that the head referred to is the one we're looking for, where does this take us?' said Tristan. 'Papus died in 1916.'

'Correct. Look at this story as another link in the chain.'

'There is more?' said Jack.

'Yes. And it gets even better,' said Cybil, enjoying herself. 'A few years before he died, Papus befriended a French materialisation medium, Marthe Béraud—'

'Who adopted the pseudonym Eva Carrière,' interjected Tristan. 'She was a very controversial figure, who was subjected to numerous experiments and examinations in connection with emanations and something called ectoplasm. Houdini attended several sessions and corresponded with Arthur Conan Doyle, who was also very interested in the occult, about what he had witnessed. Houdini wasn't convinced about Eva Carrière's honesty. Fraud was suspected.'

'Correct,' said Cybil, no longer surprised by Tristan's baffling knowledge of occult subjects. 'But back to the talking head. This brings us to the records of the Society for Psychical Research and a review of Eva Carrière published in 1915. There is mention of a tattooed head being used during one of the séances and we've found a reference in one of Eva's letters, where she mentions a gift from Papus and refers to a tattooed human head with special powers.'

Jack raised an eyebrow. 'The next link in the chain?' he said.

'Precisely. We believe that we can now place the fifth Robley *Mokomokai* bought by Oldfield, with Eva Carrière in about 1915 or so. And this brings me to Madame Lumière,' said Cybil, leaning back in her comfortable wicker chair. 'Around 1939, Carrière formed a friendship with a young French clairvoyant who called herself Madame Lumière and had become very popular in Paris society circles.'

'Tell us about her,' said Isis, enjoying her third glass of champagne.

'Madame Lumière had a *salon spirituelle* right here in Paris. Not far from here, actually,' said Cybil. 'She gave tarot readings in the afternoon, followed by séances in the evening, which were often attended by the same clients. The séances, in particular, were very popular and you had to book several weeks in advance to be able to participate. Because Eva Carrière was already well known in Paris, Madame Lumière joined forces with her from time to time, and they gave séances together, which were quite the rage with the occult-dabbling set, always on the lookout for excitement and the next spiritual adventure. Lumière and Carrière became very close and it was rumoured they were more than just friends ...'

'Fascinating,' said Jack. 'But where is this link taking us?' he said, the impatience in his tone apparent.

'To the Second World War and the German occupation of Paris.'

'Intriguing,' said Isis. 'Here come our entrées now.'

Cybil waited until the waiter had left the table before continuing.

'This arrangement continued until the Germans marched into Paris in June 1940. After that, life changed. Lumière and Carrière drifted apart, and Carrière died in 1943. Lumière, on the other hand, was a resourceful survivor. She made contact with the Germans and befriended a high-ranking officer who lived in the Ritz, which was the German headquarters here in Paris at the time. But you know all about the Ritz, don't you, Jack?' said Cybil.

'He sure does,' said Isis. 'The Ritz and its colourful wartime occupants feature prominently in his books.'

'Yes, *The Hidden Genes of Professor K* and *The Lost Symphony*,' said Jack, wondering where all this was heading.

'To cut a long story short, Lumière moved into the Ritz, and the tattooed "talking" head moved in with her.'

'Are you serious?' said Jack.

'Absolutely. We have ample material to back this up. But let's eat first, and I'll tell you more a little later.'

'Good idea,' said Jack, and tucked into his entrée with gusto.

'The Nazi love affair with the occult is well known,' began Cybil after the table had been cleared. 'Himmler, in particular, was a fervent occultist, and Goehring wasn't far behind. The Reichsmarschall arranged numerous séances at the Ritz for his cronies, and enjoyed dressing up for the occasion. Lumière was in her element and exploited this situation to the fullest.'

'Like that incredible crystal skull?' said Jack. 'There was even a scandal about that.'

'Yes. The Ritz was a hotbed of intrigue, with lavish parties, drugs, and debauchery on a scale difficult to imagine,' said Cybil. 'And Lumière and her tattooed head were right in the middle of it all and became a much-talked-about curiosity. We have found a lot of material documenting this, even a photo.'

Cybil held up a photograph, and then passed it around. It was a picture of a tattooed human head balancing on what looked like a large crystal.

'Definitely looks like the head we're after,' said Tristan. 'The *moko*, especially here on the forehead, is just like the one in the Goldie portrait.'

Tristan handed the photo to Jack. 'What do you think?'

Jack looked at the photo and nodded. 'You're right. Do we know what happened to it?' he asked, cutting to the chase.

Cybil realised she was reaching the pointy end of the conversation and decided to get quickly to the issues that mattered. 'Yes, and no,' she said. 'Lumière and her German lover stayed at the Ritz until the Germans evacuated Paris in August 1944. By then she had given birth to a son, Joachim. Her lover went back to Germany, but Lumière stayed in Paris with her son, which couldn't have been easy. The Resistance was hunting down collaborateurs like her. Do you know what these women who slept with the Nazis during the occupation were called?'

'Horizontals,' said Jack. 'I think we know why.'

'Exactly. Unfortunately, the Lumière trail went cold after the Germans left. Lumière went to live in Montmartre with a sister for a while, and then went to ground and just disappeared with her son.'

'Is this it?' asked Tristan, frowning.

'You can do this much better than me, Richard,' said Cybil, turning to her husband. 'After all, you found Cagliostro.'

'All right,' said Richard, who had been patiently waiting his turn.

'*Cagliostro?*' said Jack. 'Not the famous eighteenth-century Italian magician who dabbled in the occult?'

'No, of course not, but someone who used his name as an alias. Just when we thought we had finally hit a brick wall with our investigation, I came across a French newspaper article in one of the files.' Richard reached for the manila folder on the table. 'This is it here,' he said and held up a piece of paper. 'Written by an investigative journalist in 2016.'

'What's it about?' said Isis.

'It's all about a scandal involving French politicians and under-aged girls. Apparently, the police raided a party after receiving a tip-off about drugs and other illegal activities. The party turned out to be some kind of dodgy séance in the ruins of a chateau, attended by some senior politicians and other notables. No names are mentioned, but in essence, the séance was apparently nothing more than an orgy involving under-aged girls, drugs, and dubious occult practices arranged by a shady character who called himself Cagliostro. So far, there's nothing of particular interest to us in all this except for two things: a name, and something else.'

'A name? What name?' said Jack.

'The article went on to say that Cagliostro was a notorious occultist and fraudster, well known for arranging questionable parties he called séances.' Richard paused, and looked around the table. 'Now comes the interesting bit,' he said, lowering his voice. 'The journalist speculated that Cagliostro could be an alias for Jean-Baptiste Lafayette, a convicted criminal who had spent several years in jail. It was this name that caught my attention.'

'Why?' said Tristan.

'Because Lumière's *real* name was Bernadette Lafayette, and it occurred to me that there had to be a connection. As it turned out, I was right. Jean-Baptiste Lafayette is none other than Lumière's grandson. The boy, Joachim, born at the Ritz during the war, was his father,' said Richard, beaming.

'Wow! That's quite a discovery. Well done! No wonder you wanted to meet with us and tell us about it,' said Jack.

'And the other thing that caught your attention?' asked Tristan.

'Ah. That was about questionable occult practices involving—'

'Yes?' prompted Isis.

'A grotesque, tattooed human head that could *talk*!'

'What?' Jack almost shouted. 'The final link in the chain?'

'Could be. Needless to say, we made further inquiries about Lafayette. Police and court records, mainly. Even after his arrest in 2018 – unrelated to the scandal I mentioned earlier – and doing time, Lafayette returned to his usual shady activities and spent more time in jail for similar offences. Drugs, fraud, prostitution, stuff like that, but all somehow linked to questionable occult practices, often involving women who acted as mediums and were his partners – in crime, I suppose. And, of course, somehow always using a talking human head as the main drawcard.'

'Inherited from his grandmother, perhaps?' suggested Tristan.

'Who knows?' said Cybil.

'Astonishing. So, what are you suggesting?' said Jack.

'What I am suggesting is this: based on the evidence so far, we can say with some degree of confidence that in 2016, the year of the article, it would appear that an occultist who called himself Cagliostro was using a tattooed human head as part of a séance performance, which resulted in a scandal. The point of real interest to us is the suggestion that Cagliostro could have been an alias for Jean-Baptiste Lafayette, a petty criminal involved in dubious occult practices. We also know that Lafayette continued these occult practices after his arrest in 2018, right up to the present. When he wasn't in jail, that is, which was often. It therefore stands to reason that he may still have the head we're looking for in his possession, and is using it during his séances. You know what they say; a leopard …'

'If you're right, it follows that if we find Lafayette, we'll most likely find the missing head. Is that what you are saying?' asked Tristan.

'Yes, that's the logical conclusion to this long, fascinating line of inquiry,' said Richard. 'It's also our best, no, our *only*, lead we have left.'

'I can see that,' said Jack. 'So, where to from here?'

'French police and court records are notoriously difficult to get access to, especially for foreigners like us,' said Cybil. 'However, by calling in favours we have been able to establish that Lafayette has recently been released from prison and is currently on parole. But before you get too excited, we have no idea where he is. To find out, we would need contacts in the French police, which we do not have, but we believe you do, Jack?'

'He sure does,' said Isis. 'Right to the top.'

'What Cybil and I are proposing is collaboration here,' said Richard. 'We continue with our inquiries and stay involved, but you turn to your police contacts here to find out more about Lafayette and his whereabouts. This would save a lot of time and considerably improve our chances.'

Jack locked eyes with Tristan sitting opposite. 'What do you think?'

'Dupree?'

'Who else?'

'Who's Dupree?' asked Richard.

'A retired French police officer we've worked with before. Well connected, right up the chain of command. He lives on the Kuragin estate, where we're heading after this. Mademoiselle Darrieux, who arranged the reservation here, insisted we come and stay the night at the chateau, a high-end boutique hotel she's managing. She's even sending a car to pick us up.'

'And she doesn't take no for an answer,' said Isis, laughing. 'As Jack well knows ...'

'No, she doesn't.' Jack looked at his watch. 'In fact, François, the Kuragin chauffeur, should arrive shortly.'

'A private plane to get here, and a chauffeur-driven car to take you to an exclusive chateau after lunch to spend the night? Not bad. What do you think, Cybil?' said Richard.

Jack shrugged. 'I'm a lucky guy,' he said.

'He is that,' said Lola, 'and a lot more.'

'Friends in the right places,' said Tristan.

Jack looked at Richard. 'Where are you staying? Can we give you a lift?'

'No, thank you. We're staying in a small hotel not far from here.'

'You and Cybil have done an outstanding job,' said Jack, 'and in such a short time. Remarkable. Thank you. No wonder Isis said you were the best in the business.'

'You're welcome,' said Richard, well pleased by the compliment.

'We'll talk to Dupree tonight. Let's take it from there.'

'We'll find the head,' said Tristan softly.

'What makes you say that?' asked Isis.

'As soon as I heard the name Lafayette mentioned, I knew it was the missing link.'

Just then, the Maître d' came over to the table. 'Monsieur Rogan?' Jack held up his hand. 'Your car is waiting outside.'

'We must do this again,' said Jack. He stood up and turned to Isis. 'We can drop you off at the airport, if you like?'

Isis drained her glass and stood up as well. 'Perfect. Let's go. I had no idea that looking for *Mokomokai* could be this much fun; did you, Tristan?'

'I wouldn't call it fun. Destiny, more like.'

Kuragin chateau, just outside Paris: 14 October

As soon as the car crossed the little bridge over the moat leading to the chateau, Jack began to relax. The familiar surroundings conjured up precious memories of good times and friendships forged during a turbulent period in his life. It was the place where Tristan had found a home after his mother had been tragically killed protecting Anna, Countess Kuragin's daughter, in a hospital in Broome. It was the place where Tristan had grown up and gone to school, and found the warm embrace of a grateful family.

It was also the place where Jack had done some of his best writing, especially in winter, when the snow-covered trees reminded him of old men in fur coats, drifting out of the morning fog like the scary giants in Russian fairytales.

'I do miss this place,' said Tristan as the car pulled up at the entrance.

'So do I,' said Jack. 'But nothing stands still, and some things never change. Like Adrienne's car. There, *look!*' Jack pointed to the 1980 Citroën 2CV, a classic, parked between a Maserati and a Rolls Royce, which obviously belonged to well-heeled guests.

'She loves that car,' said François. 'Just as well. She's a terrible driver. At least this way, everyone sees her coming and can move out of the way. Ah, here she comes.'

Mademoiselle Darrieux, celebrated author and Paris socialite, swept down the stairs to greet them, her generous proportions squeezed into a far-too-tight designer outfit, designed for women half her age.

'What took you so long? Cook's been worried sick. She's been fussing for hours in the kitchen over your favourite dinner, Jack. Great to see you, guys.'

Tristan winced as Darrieux gave him a chest-crushing hug and planted a kiss on both his cheeks. He locked eyes with Jack and winked. '*Food again,*' he whispered. '*I don't know how you do it.*'

'Come, let's go straight down into the kitchen. Hopefully, just in time to avoid a culinary disaster. We were supposed to eat half an hour ago.'

'What's for dinner?' asked Jack as he followed Darrieux down the well-worn marble stairs leading to the spacious, vaulted kitchen with its large fireplace, which had been his favourite hangout in the chateau for years. Especially late at night after everyone had gone to bed, a perfect time to raid the delicious teacake usually left on the table by Antoinette, the cook, for starving night owls.

'Steak-and-kidney pie; what else?'

'Did you hear that, Tristan? Real food at last.'

After an enthusiastic welcome by Antoinette, Jack and Tristan took their usual seats at the large wooden refectory table. Jack smiled as he noticed two bottles of Louis Jadot Corton Grand Cru Burgundy, his favourite French red wine, next to the old samovar – a family heirloom – in the middle of the large table. *'A tea urn warming generations' as Katerina used to call it*, thought Jack and reached for his napkin. Moments later, dinner was served.

Antoinette took off her apron and joined them. 'Let's eat first, and then you can tell us all about what brought you here in such a hurry. Not clowns again, I hope.' This was a reference to a tense situation a few years earlier when two armed men wearing clown masks had burst into the chateau, causing mayhem.

'Nothing like that, but we do want to talk to Claude as soon as possible.'

Jack had phoned Dupree after lunch and given him some background information about Lafayette. Dupree promised to make inquiries straight away and seemed pleased to have been asked.

'Sounds ominous,' said Darrieux. 'He's in the cottage waiting for you. He's been on the phone all afternoon. I don't know, but shady characters and danger seem to follow you wherever you go.'

'Don't blame me,' said Jack. 'This is all Tristan's doing. I'm just along for the ride.'

'Sure. A little more wine, anyone?'

After dinner, Jack and Tristan walked over to the Gatekeeper's Cottage next to the bridge to meet Claude Dupree, a retired police officer. Since the house fire that had destroyed his home in Montmartre and killed his son in 2017, Dupree had been living in the cottage, which Countess Kuragin had made available for him. Since then, Dupree, a long-time friend, had become a member of the extended Kuragin family and had shared several memorable escapades with Jack and Tristan.

Dupree put a bottle of cognac on the table in front of the fireplace. 'Help yourself, guys,' he said, clearly pleased to see Jack and Tristan. 'It's been a while.'

'Sure has,' said Jack and poured himself a drink.

'So, you finally got away from Adrienne?'

'She means well.'

'She does, but her enthusiasm can be a little overwhelming at times, just like her outfits.'

'How true,' said Tristan.

'That's why I stayed away from dinner; otherwise, we would still be in the kitchen, drinking Cointreau on ice,' said Dupree, laughing. 'And besides, I did put the time to good use.'

'Regarding Lafayette?' said Jack.

'Yes.'

'Any luck?' asked Tristan.

'Let's put it this way: we've made a start.'

Jack reached for his glass. 'Can't wait to hear what you have to tell us. *Santé!*'

'It's been a little quiet around here since our last little encounter with the underworld,' said Dupree.

'We sure wouldn't want to repeat that now, would we?' said Jack. 'Two dead police officers in front of your cottage, followed by an armed home invasion that almost gave Antoinette a heart attack.'

'Certainly not. Lapointe still talks about the way you managed to corner O'Hara in Belarus. That was something. The French police is forever in your debt; you know that.'

Jack waved dismissively.

'I already spoke to Lapointe and told him that you've asked for assistance.'

'And?'

'He made some phone calls. And when the Senior Commissaire of the Paris Brigade Criminelle makes phone calls, people listen and doors open.'

'I see.' Jack pointed to Tristan sitting opposite. 'I can also see that you're dying to ask about Tristan's tattoo.'

'I am a little curious,' admitted Dupree and poured himself another cognac.

'Tristan, why don't you tell Claude the story behind your *moko*. He hasn't been able to take his eyes off it, but is too polite to ask. Isn't that right, Claude?'

'Policeman's curiosity, that's all.'

'Sure. You should really hear this story first before we talk about Lafayette. It's the reason we're here and need your help.'

For a while there was complete silence in the room after Tristan had finished, the only sound being the evening breeze rattling the windowpanes.

'That's quite a story,' said Dupree. 'You guys always seem to come up with the unusual, to put it mildly. And you think that Lafayette could be the key here?'

'As I mentioned on the phone, he's our best lead,' said Jack. 'The end of the line. Our *only* lead, in fact.'

Dupree nodded. He had seen it all before. Often, complex investigations came down to a single question, a small piece in the puzzle, where all the fate lines intersected and held all the answers.

'Well, this is what I've been able to find out so far since you rang me this afternoon,' said Dupree.

'So, there was something behind the doors Lapointe opened for you?' said Jack, smiling.

Dupree sat back in his chair and looked at Jack. 'Judge for yourself.'

It was almost midnight by the time Jack went to his room at the back of the cottage. Dead tired after a long, eventful day, his body was screaming for sleep, but his mind was restless and alert. Instead of going to bed, he sat down at a small desk by the window, opened his notebook, and carefully went over his notes, digesting the surprising information Dupree had been able to unearth about Lafayette.

Jack did some of his best thinking that way, as possibilities and connections assaulted his brain, buzzing with creative ideas, and when that happened, he had to talk to someone he could trust, to make sure the spark wasn't lost.

Jack reached for his phone and found Francesca Bartolli's number. *Perhaps it's too late*, he thought, hesitating to press the call button. But she usually worked late, or read in bed for hours, so she kept telling him. Just as you would expect from one of the best criminal profilers in the business. 'One way to find out,' mumbled Jack and pressed the call button.

Francesca answered almost immediately. 'Hello, Jack. Must be important, judging by the hour.'

'It is. I hope I haven't woken you?'

'Of course not. This is Rome.'

'Where are you?'

'Sitting on the terrace with a glass of wine. Mum's just gone to bed, and the girls are still out with their friends. Despite the midnight curfew.'

'I see.'

'And where are you? Some exotic place on the other side of the world?'

'I was until a couple of days ago. New Zealand.'

'I was right, see? Holiday?'

'No.'

'I thought not. Where are you now?'

'Kuragin chateau. Just had a long discussion with Dupree.'

'Ah. So, this isn't a social call?'

'Not exactly.'

Bartolli began to laugh. 'Jack, you're so predictable.'

'I am?'

'Yes, you are, but don't worry, it's part of your charm. So, what's this all about?'

'Before I tell you, I would like to suggest something.'

'Sounds interesting. What exactly?'

'How would you feel about coming here for a few days?'

'Seriously? Why?'

'It was Dupree's idea. We need your help.'

'In what way?'

'To profile a notorious criminal we have to make contact with.'

'Intriguing.'

'It is. Once again, the occult is involved. In a big way.'

'Hm. I could do with a few days away.'

'I take this as a yes, then?'

'Why not? Mum can look after Biscotti. He's almost walked me to death.'

'Funny name. Who's Biscotti?'

'Our new dog. I got Mum a rescue mutt. Nothing fancy, but a real character. He's sitting here beside me, looking adoringly at me right now. Obviously hoping for a biscotti.'

'Ah. What a wonderful idea!'

'She was so distraught after her dog Paulo was poisoned, remember?'

'How could I forget? That was really dreadful. The Landru affair. See if you can get a flight to Paris tomorrow, and I'll pick you up at the airport.'

'Done. Now, are you going to tell me about—'

'That can wait. If I don't get some sleep now, I'll turn into a pumpkin,' said Jack.

'That would be interesting, but for now, you just want to keep me on the edge of my seat, right?'

'Something like that.'

'Rascal.'

'You forgot incorrigible. See you tomorrow.'

Montmartre, Paris: 15 October

Woken by the clatter of garbage bins being emptied below his bedroom window, Lafayette woke with a start. At first, he tried to ignore the unwelcome intrusion, but the annoying noise just got louder as the garbage truck backed into the laneway to collect more rubbish.

'*Merde!*' mumbled Lafayette and reached for his cigarettes on the bedside table. Inhaling deeply, he was hoping the nicotine rush would banish his throbbing headache and hangover, a leftover from another night of drinking and gambling in the sleazy bar under the flat.

Life had been tough after his recent release from prison. The only reason Lafayette had a roof over his head was because of a young woman, Lucille, a prostitute, whom he knew from before. Somehow, it had always been women who came to his rescue in the most unexpected ways. It was the story of his life.

Abandoned as a teenager by his alcoholic father and left to fend for himself on the streets of Montmartre, his grandmother had appeared out of nowhere and taken him under her wing. How she had managed to track him down was still a mystery, but suddenly, young Jean-Baptiste had a home and was going to school. That was also his first contact with the occult, which was to have a profound influence on his life. His grandmother was a psychic who worked as a medium and gave tarot readings in Montmartre.

Lafayette sat up in bed and looked around the tiny room as the first shafts of light of another grey, rainy day crept hesitantly along the grimy wooden floor, pointing accusingly, he thought, at the crumpled clothes he had dropped on the floor before falling into bed the night before.

What a mess. He had to get away from here. This can't go on, he thought as he heard the key turn in the lock. It was Lucille.

'You're up early,' she said and threw her handbag on the bed.

'Good night?' asked Lafayette.

'Not really. Apart from a couple of regulars, there were few punters around. Lousy weather.'

Lucille took off her jacket, sat down on the bed and looked at Lafayette. 'You are without doubt the most handsome man I've ever met,' she said and kissed Lafayette on the cheek. Good looks and a striking physique had been Lafayette's biggest assets. Women of all ages were drawn to him and his natural charm, something he had ruthlessly exploited during a life of petty crime.

'If you say so. I've been thinking ...'

'What about?'

Lafayette pointed to a stack of books on the floor next to the bed. Anyone looking at the titles would have been surprised. *Three Books of Occult Philosophy* by Heinrich Cornelius Agrippa, originally published in 1531; *The Divine Pymander* by Hermes Trismegistus, first published in 1657; *Isis Unveiled*, by the Russian occultist Helena P. Blatvatsky; *The New Atlantis* by Francis Bacon, published posthumously in 1626; and *The Hermetic and Alchemical Writings of Paracelsus*, were some of the books he had inherited from his grandmother and had studied in jail.

'I know a lot about the occult.'

'I know you do.'

'My grandmother made a good living out of it, especially during the war, right here in Paris.'

'So what?'

'We could too.'

'You don't believe all this occult business, do you?'

'Many do.'

'So?'

'We too could make a good living out of it. I've done it before ...'

'You told me,' said Lucille, unconvinced. 'And it landed you in jail.'

'True. But it doesn't have to be that way. I've learned my lesson.'

'I don't know anything about the occult, the tarot, séances, stuff like that.'

'I could teach you. I think you would make a wonderful medium. Men find you irresistible.'

'Don't be silly!'

'I'm serious. We could save some money and go to America. A new start. All we need is a break or two.'

'Dreamer.'

'I mean it. We have to get away from this. You can see that, surely?'

'Tell me about it.'

Lafayette picked up one of the books from the floor and held it up. It was *Beelzebub's Tales to His Grandson* by G.I. Gurdjieff. 'It's all in here in this book,' he said. 'According to some, it's one of the one hundred most influential books ever written.'

'If you say so. I believe in the here and now,' purred Lucille, slowly sticking the tip of her tongue into Lafayette's ear before reaching under the blanket.

On the way to Sainte-Anne Hospital Centre, Paris: 15 October

Charles de Gaulle Airport was chaotic as usual, with dozens of arrivals scheduled from all over Europe. Jack was making his way to the Arrivals Hall to meet Bartolli when his phone rang. It was Dupree.

'Is the plane on time?'

'Just landed. Why?'

'I just had a call from Lapointe. He wants us to meet him at the Sainte-Anne Hospital Centre.'

'Did he say why?'

'It's about Lafayette. That's all he said, but he did say it was urgent.'

'Interesting. Does Lapointe know that Francesca is now involved?'

'Yes, he does. It was one of the reasons he wants us to meet him there.'

'Where is this hospital?'

'In the 14th arrondissement. François will know the way.'

'All right. We'll get there as soon as we can.'

'By the way, Sainte-Anne's is a psychiatric hospital. See you there.'

'You're a dark horse, Jack. I drop everything, get on the first available flight to Paris to meet you, and we are going straight to a *psychiatric hospital*? Really?' said Bartolli after Jack had met her at the gate. 'Why?'

'I can't tell you much more. Dupree just called and asked if we could meet him there. Something urgent—'

'About the matter you're investigating and you decided not to tell me about last night?'

'Yes. It's about a man called Jean-Baptiste Lafayette, who has recently been released from prison.'

'The man you want me to profile?'

'Aha. I told Dupree this morning that I had asked for your help and was picking you up at the airport. He must have told Lapointe about it, and here we are.'

'All right. Let's see where this takes us,' said Bartolli, a familiar sense of excitement and anticipation washing over her.

'Thank God François is driving. Look at this traffic! Paris. I have never been able to manage it,' said Jack.

'Too much for the country boy from Australia?' said Bartolli, a sparkle in her eyes. 'Used to deserted dusty roads and distant horizons without even a single tree in the way? Mysterious criminals are easier to handle?'

'Something like that.'

'Now, are you going to tell me what this is all about?'

Jack sat back in the comfortable leather seat and looked at Bartolli.

'Sure. It all began with a phone call from New Zealand about a month ago. We were having dinner with Katerina in Venice when Tristan received a call. It all went from there ...'

While François was threading his way through the busy Paris traffic, Jack told Bartolli about the relationship between Tristan and the Bone Scraper, and Tristan's fateful promise just before his uncle died. He explained who Parema Te Pahau was, and what finding the tattooed head would mean to Tristan.

'Please understand that all this is only background information, which will put what I am about to tell you now into context. It explains why we're interested in Lafayette, and why we want to find him.'

'Okay.'

'But to be able to do that, you have to hear what Dupree told me about Lafayette last night, because that's why I asked you to come here and help us.'

'Understood,' said Bartolli, used to quick briefings on the run.

Jack opened his notebook and looked at the cryptic bullet-point entries he had scribbled down the night before, which only he could decipher. 'This is what we know about the man so far ...'

'How old is he?'

'Late forties. His father was born right here in Paris in 1944 during the German occupation. War baby. French mother, Nazi father. Both were living in the Ritz at the time but parted company when the Germans evacuated Paris.'

'Fascinating. Echoes of the crystal skull scandal, and the Landru affair?'

'Very good. In more ways than you may think,' said Jack, pleased by the way Bartolli had immediately made the connection. 'Tristan would call it destiny.'

'He sees things differently.'

'Sure does. Isis is involved in this as well,' continued Jack.

'Why am I not surprised? You certainly have an eclectic team of sleuths available whom you can call on.'

'May I consider you one of the team?'

'Let's hear what you have to tell me first.'

'Fair enough. You know how well connected Isis is in all matters involving art. Stuff like that?'

'Sure. *The Forgotten Painting* – the Monet affair – was an excellent example.'

'It was indeed. Well, Isis brought in one of her old contacts, the Craigieburns, a husband-and-wife team, to help us locate Parema Te Pahau's tattooed head, which ended up in a collection of an English major general after having been traded for muskets during the Musket Wars in New Zealand.'

'A well-travelled head, wouldn't you say?' said Bartolli, wondering where this was heading.

'Quite. They came up with some surprising results in record time. Here in Paris, actually.'

'What kind of results?'

'In essence, they came up with a name: Jean-Baptiste Lafayette, a petty criminal with a long record.'

'What kind of record?'

'Drugs, theft and fraud mainly, but always somehow involving the occult. Lafayette has been in and out of prison since his teens. Habitual criminal.'

'Sounds straightforward. So, why do you need me?'

'Ah. That's about something else. Don't forget, our interest in all this is finding the tattooed Māori head.'

'You told me.'

'It would appear that Lafayette has been living a double life.'

'In what way?'

'Well, on the one hand, we have the petty criminal I just described—'

'And on the other?'

'Seems to be something more sinister and complicated, but once again associated with the occult. The Craigieburns discovered a possible connection between someone who called himself Cagliostro, and Lafayette. If the Craigieburns are right, and their source is reliable, then Cagliostro and Lafayette are one and the same person, but with a very different persona and modus operandi.'

'And this tenuous connection is important to your investigation?'

'Yes, it is.'

'Why?'

'Because apart from booze, drugs, and scantily clad female mediums prepared to do a little more than just reading tarot cards and making contact with the departed if the money was right, Cagliostro's exotic séances were famous for one other rather extraordinary thing.'

'What?'

'Something that made them very popular with the well-heeled Parisian social set, always on the lookout for the next adventure, however depraved.'

'Are you going to tell me what that was, or just keep me dangling on the edge of curiosity?'

'A talking tattooed human head that could speak and make contact with the spirit world.'

'Seriously?'

'Yes. This was sending the Paris occult-hungry socialites into quite a spin at the time. Cagliostro's séances were all the rage. The sessions were booked out weeks in advance, with eye-watering entry fees only the very rich could afford. Hardly the modus operandi of a petty criminal, wouldn't you say?'

'Certainly not. When was this?'

'In 2016.'

'And then these séances just stopped?'

'Apparently so.'

'Do you know why?'

'Not yet. There's obviously a lot more we need to find out about all this.'

'Understood. And Dupree is helping you?'

'He is. Tristan was very excited when he heard the name Lafayette. He could sense that we are on the right track here and getting close.'

Bartolli nodded. She knew better than to dismiss Tristan's intuition as unscientific speculation. She had seen it work in astonishing ways before.

'You can therefore imagine our excitement when we heard this. And, it gets better,' said Jack.

'It does?'

'Yes. The Craigieburns made another important connection.'

'What kind of connection?'

'Lafayette is not a common name. They were able to establish a connection between a notorious Frenchwoman who called herself Madame Lumière and lived in the Ritz during the German occupation, fraternising with the Nazis. We have been able to trace the Māori head we're looking for to Madame Lumière; she was a famous French occultist who used the tattooed head in her séances. Apparently, Jean-Baptiste Lafayette is her grandson.'

Silence.

'I see,' said Bartolli at last. 'So, this is the brief: we are trying to locate Lafayette – a petty criminal who has recently been released from jail – to find out if he and Cagliostro, who was the impresario of extravagant séances seven or so years ago, using a tattooed talking human head to make contact with the spirit world, are one and the same person. How am I doing so far?'

'Very well.'

'And the reason we're doing all this?' asked Bartolli.

'If Lafayette and Cagliostro are in fact the same person, then we have a credible link to Madame Lumière and the Māori head we're looking for.'

'And you're hoping that Lafayette still has it, or knows what happened to it, right?'

'Spot on, as usual.'

'Are you serious? This is the longest long shot I've ever seen.'

'I've seen worse,' said Jack, looking a little sheepish.

'Come on, Jack, even by your standards this is a wild goose chase, and you know it.'

'Finding Tchaikovsky's lost symphony and Van Eyck's stolen altarpiece was much worse, I can tell you.'

Unconvinced, Bartolli shook her head.

'I'm sorry you see it that way,' said Jack. 'At least give me a chance to change your mind. You know Lapointe better than me. He wouldn't have asked us to meet him in a hurry if it wasn't important. And it's all about Lafayette. At least let's hear what he has to say, and we'll take it from there.'

'All right, Jack. Let's do that. At least I got away from Biscotti and the girls for a couple of days, even if my forensic skills may be wasted here.'

Jack reached for Bartolli's hand and squeezed it. 'I'll make it up to you; promise.'

Bartolli sat back, laughing. 'I'm sure you will, Jack. Incorrigible rascals always do.'

Jack pointed out the car window. 'Look, here we are. Didn't take that long after all.'

Meeting Dr Garnier; Sainte-Anne Hospital Centre: 15 October

Jack walked into the imposing foyer of the historical Sainte-Anne Hospital Centre and smiled as he recognised a familiar figure standing next to Dupree by the stairs. Seeing Detective Chief Superintendent Lapointe always reminded Jack of Maigret, the legendary fictional Paris detective who featured in more than seventy novels by Georges Simenon, a Belgian writer, and became an iconic character and the subject of countless films and TV dramas.

Shortish, powerfully built, and wearing a heavy overcoat and his black fedora he always carried with him, he rarely attracted attention and liked it that way, because staying in the shadows was the best way to observe and analyse the dark side of life.

While his appearance may have been unremarkable, his face wasn't. Radiating intelligence but also sadness and compassion, the eyes had seen a little too much brutality and violence, and the deep lines around his mouth and prominent chin suggested a determination to do something about it.

Lapointe greeted Jack like an old friend, and then extended his hand to greet Bartolli.

'So glad you could come, Professor,' said Lapointe. 'Most opportune, as you will see in a moment. I have never forgotten your involvement in the Landru case and the consequences of ignoring your opinions and advice. I am determined not to make the same mistake again.'

'Do you think this matter could in some way be similar?' asked Jack.

Lapointe shrugged. 'Let's take a walk in the gardens before I introduce you to Dr Garnier, one of our most prominent psychoanalysts and psychiatrists.'

'Dr Garnier is *here*?' said Bartolli, surprised.

'Yes, he's a consultant here in the Psychiatric Infirmary of the Police Department, which is run by the Paris Police Prefecture.'

'We used to study his work when I was at university in Rome. It was like a forensic bible of human nature. He must be quite elderly?'

'He is. With knowledge and experience of a lifetime behind him. That's why we're here,' said Lapointe and pointed to the doors. 'Shall we?'

'What a stunning place,' said Jack as they walked into the expansive, manicured gardens.

'Sure is,' said Dupree. 'One of our finest institutions, with a long history going all the way back to the seventeenth century. However, it was Napoleon III who created a psychiatric hospital here for treating mental illness in 1863, and it all went from there. Very innovative and far-sighted for the times.'

Lapointe pulled his pipe out of his coat pocket and lit it.

'You must be wondering why I asked you to meet me here,' he said. 'As you will see in a moment, there are good reasons for this and it all has to do with Lafayette, and something Claude mentioned in passing on the phone yesterday. That was the spark that ignited all this. Or reignited, would be a better way to put it.'

'Intriguing,' said Jack, his curiosity aroused.

Lapointe turned to Bartolli standing next to him. 'You would know all about sparks igniting curiosity, and curiosity opening unexpected doors, showing us possibilities and connections that would never have occurred to us without that moment of inspiration, wouldn't you, Professor?'

'Quite so. And are you suggesting the matter that brought us here could represent something like that?'

'I would like you to make up your own mind once you've heard what Dr Garnier has to say.'

'Very well.'

Dr Garnier was waiting in his spacious office on the first floor overlooking the garden. Since his second stroke a year earlier, he had been confined to a wheelchair but had fully regained his speech. He reminded Jack of Professor Stolzfus, sitting in his wheelchair in Oxford as the newly appointed Lucasian Professor of Mathematics, only older. Same frail body, looking almost comical in a three-piece suit and bowtie, but with a face that was both expressive and captivating.

Bartolli gasped as soon as she set eyes on Dr Garnier sitting in his wheelchair by the window. Deeply affected by the obvious ravages of age – Dr Garnier was in his high eighties – she tried to remember the man in the video masterclasses she used to watch at university. However, as soon as she heard him speak, the cloud of mortality lifted, allowing an extraordinary mind to shine through, because Dr Garnier's voice hadn't changed at all.

'Professor Bartolli, what a pleasure to meet you,' said Garnier after Lapointe had made the introductions. 'I have read a number of your papers over the years. Remarkable. You have a wonderful way of applying theory and deduction to facts and making them not only relevant, but also revealing what is often hidden by the complexities of human nature and behaviour.'

'Thank you, Doctor. I have learned most of what I know about the criminal mind from you,' said Bartolli, a little taken aback by the compliment.

Garnier turned his wheelchair around and looked out the window.

'There were some very famous patients in here over the years,' he said. 'Many of them were poets and writers. For instance, the famous poet Antonin Artaud spent time here during the 1930s, and so did the philosopher Louis Althusser. The surrealist designer and poet Unica Zürn was treated here at Sainte-Anne's as well, before she sadly committed suicide by jumping out of her Paris apartment window.'

'I didn't know that,' said Jack. 'She was the author of *Der Mann im Jasmin*, and *Dunkler Frühling*. Quite a trailblazer.'

Impressed, Dr Garnier turned around and looked at Jack. 'You are well informed, Mr Rogan. Mental illness can have devastating conse-quences, especially when the criminal mind is involved. The line between madness and creative genius, between right and wrong, can be very blurred at times.'

'Is that what you found when you examined Lafayette?' asked Lapointe, trying to steer the conversation towards the subject that had brought them all together that morning.

'It was more complicated than that. In many ways, Lafayette was a unique and fascinating case.' Garnier began to riffle through a bundle of papers on a small table next to his wheelchair. 'It's all in my report here.'

'Like Anielka?' said Lapointe, watching Jack carefully.

'No, Anielka was in a category quite of her own,' said Garnier. 'A most incredible case with a very tragic ending, as I recall it.'

'Mr Rogan knows all about that. He was there when she died,' said Lapointe.

Shocked, Jack looked at Garnier. 'Anielka was here?'

'Yes. I treated her.'

Oh my God! Thought Jack as he remembered one of the most incredible women he had ever met, a cold shiver racing down his spine as painful memories came flooding back and began to claw at his heart.

'You were there when she died?' said Garnier. 'How interesting. Could you—'

'Perhaps another time,' said Jack. 'We should really talk about Lafayette …'

'Quite right.'

'Before we go into that, allow me to provide some background, which will make it easier for us to follow and understand your findings,' said Lapointe.

'By all means,' replied Garnier.

'The reason we are here is because of something you said to me yesterday, Claude,' continued Lapointe, turning to his old mentor and friend. Dupree and Lapointe had worked together for years, before Dupree retired from the police force and Lapointe went on to become Detective Chief Superintendent.

'What was that, exactly?' asked Dupree.

'You mentioned there was a possible connection between Lafayette and Cagliostro, and that it was this connection that had made Jack so interested in Lafayette. It was the reason he wanted to find him, remember?'

'Correct.'

Lapointe took off his coat and placed it carefully on an empty chair next to his hat. 'I will take a leaf out of your book, Jack, and tell you a story about a case that has troubled me for years.'

'What has been so troubling about it?' asked Jack, his curiosity aroused.

'Everything. We are talking about a bizarre, unsolved murder case with regrettable, far-reaching consequences that have weighed heavily on my conscience, and have cast a shadow over my career.'

Dupree looked at Lapointe, surprised. He had never heard him talk about personal matters like this before, especially matters involving his work. Known as an intensely private person, Lapointe rarely opened up and confided even in his closest friends.

'Sounds intriguing,' said Bartolli, watching Lapointe with interest.

'So, let's travel back to October 2016. The police received a tip-off about some suspicious activity involving drugs and other matters taking place in the ruins of an abandoned chateau just outside Paris. The tip-off alleged that some high-profile individuals were involved. The judiciary and the police force were specifically mentioned. When the local police patrol – two young officers – went to investigate, they found several expensive cars parked at the end of a dirt road in a remote, isolated place, surrounded by dense forest. They could see lights in the distance and hear music …'

The séance in the ruins just outside Paris: 16 October 2016

Cagliostro looked through a crack in the ivy-covered, crumbling sandstone wall and smiled. The attendance was better than expected. It would be a bumper night again. His sponsors would be pleased.

He called them 'sponsors' but in reality, they were dangerous people operating in the shadows, to whom he owed a lot of gambling and drug money. They had found a way for him to pay off his debts and do their bidding. This involved being the frontman for these 'special events' as they were called, involving séances, the occult, and a lot more.

As Cagliostro had dabbled in such matters before, he was the ideal choice for a frontman and, if necessary, a fall guy. But what Cagliostro didn't know was that these events had another, more sinister purpose that had nothing to do with the obvious.

It was a clear, balmy October night, and the full moon was an unexpected bonus. Perfect conditions for a foray into the supernatural to make contact with spirits residing in the afterlife, but with a little naughty fun in the here and now to spice things up along the way.

Cagliostro turned to Monique, his young assistant. Bare-breasted and wearing a black skirt too short to leave much to the imagination, but with her face hidden behind an exquisite gold Venetian Clorinda mask that gave her a mysterious, exotic appearance, she was the perfect hostess for such an exclusive event. Because she radiated excitement and temptation, she was sure to beguile the guests and make them wonder about the possibilities the night might offer. And there was certainly a lot on offer to tempt even the most jaded and discerning guest, expecting something special for the eye-watering, upfront participation payment that had to be made weeks in advance.

'Ready?'

'Yes. The guests are all seated.'

'Are they wearing their capes and the Bauta Tricorno?'

The *bauta*, the famous white Venetian carnival mask with the black tricorn hat, ensured anonymity and added mystique to the evening, because everyone looked the same, especially by candlelight, which apart from the moon was the only source of light in the ruins. The *bauta* costume had a long history, especially in Venice where it had erased class differences and allowed nobles and commoners alike to mingle and indulge in immoral behaviour, and freely dabble in vice under the cloak of anonymity. Literally.

'Yes, just as you asked. Most of them have been with us before and know the drill.'

'Good. And the girls?'

'Already in full swing. It didn't take them long to hook up with some of the regulars. The young ones especially seem to be in great demand.'

'Hardly surprising. And the coke?'

'Being sniffed right now. A lot of money is changing hands.'

'Excellent.' Cagliostro put on his red latex horned devil mask and placed the palms of his hands on the antique rosewood box he had brought with him. Decorated with ornate brass inlay and leather straps, the touch of the smooth lid sent shivers of excitement down his spine because he knew what was inside. It also reminded him of the many useful séance tricks he had learned from his grandmother, an accomplished practitioner of the dark arts, when he was still an impressionable teenager living on the streets of Montmartre.

'It's time,' said Cagliostro. 'Music, please.'

'Coming up.'

Cagliostro knew that an impressive entrance was key and set the tone for the entire evening. The old ruins of the castle were the perfect setting for an otherworldly spiritual performance to stimulate the imagination.

Seated in a semicircle facing a sandstone arch, the only structure of the chateau chapel still standing, and wearing identical masks and black capes, the spectators looked like mourners attending a pagan funeral.

Illuminated entirely by torches wedged into cracks in the stone walls, the archway looked like a stage in some dark medieval play.

As the first notes of Mozart's haunting *Requiem* drifted across the ancient sandstone structure from speakers concealed in the rubble, Cagliostro made his entrance. Wearing a black cape like all the guests, his frightening devil mask reflecting the candlelight, Cagliostro walked slowly over to a broken stone column and carefully placed the box on top, like some high priest preparing a sacrifice. Then he stepped away and turned around to face his audience, whirling his cape like a matador about to confront an attacking beast.

'Welcome,' he said, his deep voice behind the mask sounding otherworldly as he lifted his hands in a gesture of prayer, and then the music stopped.

Silence.

'Tonight, my friends, I invite you to come with me on a journey of discovery, where the impossible becomes possible, and the unthinkable becomes reality – if you open your minds and let your imagination and senses run free.'

Cagliostro, a seasoned performer, paused to let the tension grow.

'If you allow me to be your guide, we can even step beyond the grave and enter the spirit world. But to be able to do that, we need a medium to make that possible. As it happens, I have just such a medium right here. I have to warn you, he's a little frightening, but there's no need to be afraid.'

The silence prevailed.

'Would you like to meet him?' asked Cagliostro, already on a high from an earlier cocaine hit.

'*Yes! Yes!*' shouted the excited audience at last.

'Very well.' Cagliostro walked over to the box and pointed to it. 'Ready?' he asked.

'Ready,' chorused the spectators.

Slowly, Cagliostro opened the lid and reached inside the box, the mood of the spellbound spectators explosive, and full of anticipation and excitement.

The spectators gasped as Cagliostro lifted what looked like a tattooed human head out of the box. Clasping it by the hair, he held it up like a bizarre trophy for all to see.

'In case you are wondering, this is exactly what it looks like. A human head. It once belonged to a Māori warrior killed in battle, who was able to communicate with the spirit world. And he can still do so now if you listen carefully, and follow my instructions.'

Cagliostro pointed to his assistant, and then stepped into the shadows.

'If you would like to ask the medium some questions, please don't hesitate; now's the time,' said Monique. 'But be prepared. The answers may not be what you expect, or would like to hear.'

Someone in the back row stood up and pushed the girl sitting next to him aside.

'I have a question,' said the man. 'My brother, Raul, died suddenly two months ago after we had a family quarrel that deeply hurt us both. I regret what has been said and would like to ask his forgiveness now, before it's too late.'

Monique nodded and placed her hands on the tattooed forehead of the medium and closed her eyes. Almost immediately, a fog-like substance began to rise out of the head's nostrils – a trick Cagliostro had taught her – like steam rising from a boiling pot.

'Ectoplasm,' said someone in the back.

'Yes, just like in the séances of Eva Carrière,' said another.

The spectators gasped as the fog obscured the head, making it appear almost lifelike.

Cagliostro, a skilful ventriloquist, was able to create the illusion that his voice was coming from the head in front of Monique some distance away. He was able to do this without moving his lips and had used this trick many times before to great effect. A gullible audience wanting to believe then did the rest.

'I forgive you,' said Cagliostro, his deep, sonorous voice echoing through the ruins, 'as long as you forgive me too.'

'I do,' said the man at the back, close to tears.

After that, several questions followed, all of which Cagliostro answered in cryptic ways that allowed for multiple interpretations. Used to walking the tightrope of deception, he knew how to blend the vague with the credible without creating doubts, which was quite a feat, bearing in mind the entire performance depended on a talking human head making contact with spirits in the afterlife.

All went well until the unexpected intruded in a spectacular way.

Those sitting at the back saw it first: two beams of torchlight creeping along the stone floor like accusing fingers reaching out of the afterlife. When someone turned around to investigate, they saw two uniformed police officers approaching.

'*Police!*' shouted someone. After that, all hell broke loose.

Cagliostro was one of the first to realise what was happening and what was at stake. Having been involved in police raids before, he knew exactly what would happen next and what he had to do to extricate himself from a compromising situation that could easily land him back in jail.

Ignoring the desperate questions thrown at him by a wide-eyed Monique, Cagliostro had only one thing on his mind: to get away. In a great hurry, he pushed Monique roughly aside and made for the head. Grabbing it with both hands, he threw it back into the box and looked at Monique staring at him, her eyes wide with fear.

'What are we going to do?' she croaked.

'Get away as fast as we can,' hissed Cagliostro. Without saying another word, he picked up the box, took a last look at the pandemonium unfolding in front of him as the guests panicked and began to scatter in all directions, and then melted into the darkness and disappeared like a ghost.

Confused and overwhelmed by the stampede, the two young police officers were unable to deal with the volatile situation. Everyone around them looked the same and was obviously trying to get away. Within moments, the entire area was deserted and all they could hear was cars starting up and tyres screeching.

'*Merde!*' said one of the officers. 'What do you think this is all about? What's happening here?'

'No idea,' said the other officer, a young woman. 'Creepy, but obviously something was going on here we were not supposed to see.'

'True. What was that? Can you hear it?'

After some static crackling, the hidden speakers came to life again, and soon Mozart's spine-chilling *Requiem* was echoing through the ruins, giving the scene a spine-chilling, surreal touch.

'I don't like this. We are obviously not alone. We need backup!' said the officer.

'What's that over there?' said her partner, pointing his torch towards the archway. 'Can you see it? There, next to the column?'

'Let's have a look.' Slowly, the officer followed the beam of light and walked through the arch, her mouth dry, her heart beating like a drum. '*Mon Dieu!*' she shrieked moments later and reached for her radio.

* * *

'To cut a long story short,' continued Lapointe, 'the two young police officers sent to investigate a strange tip-off that could easily have turned out to be just a hoax, were out of their depth, and ill-equipped to deal with this complex situation. This was further compounded by what they found at the site.'

'What did they find?' asked Jack.

'The body of a half-naked young woman with her throat cut. You can imagine ...'

'Sure can,' said Bartolli, who had been expecting something like this.

'From there, it went from bad to worse,' said Lapointe. 'Because of the remote location of the crime scene, it took Forensics quite some time to reach the site. By then, a thunderstorm had severely compromised any evidence left behind. But worse was to come.'

'What was that?' asked Dupree.

'One clever thing one of the officers who went to investigate the tip-off did was to take down the registration numbers of some of the expensive cars parked at the site. She did this as they approached because she thought finding such cars in such a remote location was strange. This turned out to be our best lead, and also the biggest headache for the murder investigation that followed.'

'Why?' asked Bartolli.

'Because of whom these cars belonged to.'

'Can you tell us more?' said Dupree.

'The tip-off was right. We had two judges, a cabinet minister, and a high-ranking police commander to deal with, not to mention an influential billionaire Paris socialite, who could afford the very best legal representation and used his clout and influence to seriously obstruct the investigation and muddy the waters.'

'And this was your case?' said Bartolli.

'Unfortunately, it was. The pressure from the very top to solve the case in a way that would keep the high-profile "parties of interest" out of the limelight was enormous. For that reason, the investigation focused on the *organiser* of the event, believed to be a man who called himself Cagliostro.'

'And?' prompted Jack.

'I know you'll find this difficult to believe, but we were unable to find him. The man had vanished without a trace. How much of this was due to certain machinations behind the scenes, we'll never know, but Cagliostro had disappeared. We have been unable to find out anything useful about who he was, or what happened to him. Until now, that is.'

'Wow! That's quite a story,' said Jack. 'So, where to from here?'

Lapointe pointed to Dr Garnier, who had been listening in silence. 'If the information you have uncovered, Jack, is correct,' continued Lapointe, 'and there is in fact a connection between Cagliostro and Lafayette, then this could turn out to be the breakthrough I have been hoping for. In order to be able to assess this meaningfully, we should hear what Dr Garnier has to tell us about Lafayette.'

'I agree,' said Bartolli, unable to control her excitement because just like Jack, she could see another exciting case unfolding ...

Kuragin chateau: 15 October

Jack sat in his usual wicker chair by the window in the conservatory, where he had done a lot of writing over the years. After the refectory table in the kitchen it was his favourite place in the chateau, where he was comfortable and felt at ease, surrounded by exotic palms and ferns that reminded him of sunny Queensland.

Jack looked up when Bartolli walked in.

'How did he take it?' she asked. 'I saw you strolling through the garden together.'

'He didn't seem surprised.'

'You told him everything that transpired during this extraordinary meeting with Lapointe and Dr Garnier?'

'I did. I gained the impression that somehow he already knew all about it and was a step ahead of us in what we should do next.'

'Remarkable.'

'As I told you, I think his powers are getting stronger. He's more confident and perceptive than ever with his insights. He's a psychic somnambulist walking the tightrope between intuition and reality. He scares me at times.'

'I can understand that. You two are very close.'

'We are.'

'So, what did you make of what Garnier told us?'

'I was about to ask you the same thing.'

Bartolli smiled. 'You first.'

'All right, but before we do that, let's have a look at what we've got so far.'

Jack reached for his notebook and opened it.

'Good idea,' said Bartolli. She pulled a chair across to the window and sat down next to Jack. 'It's so peaceful here. Stunning view. A pond with water lilies and ducks, surrounded by willows; idyllic.'

'A great place to let your imagination run free,' said Jack, looking dreamily out of the window.

'Good, because imagination is precisely what we need – lots of it – if we want to solve this case and help Tristan find the head.'

'I agree.'

'You've never been short in that department, Jack. Using your imagination, I mean.'

Jack shrugged. 'That's what writers do.'

'True, but you can use imagination to solve problems in the real world.'

'Isn't that what you do?'

'Not exactly. My methods are scientific, analytical if you like. *Logical.*'

'And mine are not?'

'Not always. You follow a hunch, Jack. Very effectively, I might add. And then you're like a dog with a bone. I've seen you do it many times. I, on the other hand, deal with facts.'

'You're right. And Tristan? How does he approach such challenges, do you think?'

'Ah. Now that's something entirely different again. Tristan's a creature of *intuition*, which has nothing to do with scientific method or analysis. It goes beyond all that. What he has is something you cannot learn. It's a gift.'

'And do you believe it works?'

'Oh, yes. It sure does. Often, spectacularly so.'

'Coming from you, this really means something. And how do we explain this? Scientifically, I mean?'

'We can't. But at the same time it would be foolish to ignore it, because it's real. The human mind is a strange place and often works in mysterious ways we don't quite understand.'

'Very well. Are you suggesting that if the three of us work together and bring our respective talents to the table, we could make some headway here?'

'Absolutely.'

'In that case, let's do that. Give me a moment; I'll ask Tristan to join us.'

'Good idea. Why don't you ask Claude as well? May I have a drink, please?'

'Sure. What would you like?'

'Gin and Tonic?'

'Coming up.'

Bartolli had almost finished her G&T by the time Tristan and Dupree walked in. 'I think we should take stock of what we've found out so far while everything is still fresh in our minds and not diluted by too much analysis and interpretation,' she said. 'And speculation; the worst offender by far.'

'Good idea,' said Tristan and turned to Jack. 'You're the methodical one here, with the notes. Why don't you give us a summary?'

'All right,' said Jack and reached for his notebook. 'Let's go back to the beginning, as far as Lafayette is concerned. It all began with a chance discovery by the Craigieburns a few days ago. They found a Paris newspaper article about a scandal involving a séance in 2016. This séance, which involved drugs, under-aged girls and a lot more, was arranged by an occultist who called himself Cagliostro and was attended by some high-profile individuals.'

Jack paused and had a closer look at some of the entries in his notebook, in an attempt to decipher his own scribble.

'What is of particular interest to us,' continued Jack, 'is the suggestion in the article – without any evidence, I might add – that Cagliostro could have been an alias for Jean-Baptiste Lafayette, a petty criminal known for dabbling in the occult and arranging dubious séances involving a talking tattooed human head.'

'So far, so good,' said Bartolli. 'But don't you think it strange that this article makes no mention of the murder of the young woman Lapointe told us about?'

'Not necessarily. Don't forget, Lapointe said that this murder was hushed up at the time, and there was huge pressure from above to keep the "parties of interest", as he called them, out of the investigation and away from the press. However, what I do find curious,' said Jack, 'is that Cagliostro just disappeared and was never found. Sounds convenient, doesn't it?'

'This kind of thing has happened before,' said Dupree. 'Powerful people go to incredible lengths to protect reputations. Because of the people involved, I think the police just wanted to close the case and bury it. And that is exactly what seems to have happened.'

'And according to Lapointe, there was a good reason for this, remember?' said Bartolli.

'I'm coming to that,' said Jack, holding up his hand. 'You're right, there was. The police soon formed the view that Cagliostro, whoever he was, couldn't have acted alone. The way the séance had been arranged was far too complex and sophisticated for just one man and a few young prostitutes. There had to have been accomplices with contacts in high places and resources to make it all work.'

'Correct,' said Bartolli. 'And Lapointe – being the thorough and capable investigator he is – soon came up with a credible, persuasive scenario: he said he'd found evidence that the Mafia was behind it all. And he told us why, didn't he?'

'Yes,' said Dupree. 'And it certainly wasn't money. It was something far more valuable and sinister. If Lapointe is right, it involved a court case, a high-ranking police officer, and a judge. Both the officer and the judge attended the séance and found themselves in a highly compromising situation, which the Mafia had orchestrated and was ready to exploit. In short, the séance was a trap. A drug-fuelled honey trap made even more deadly by the murder of one of the prostitutes involved, moments before the police arrived at the scene. That takes some planning.'

'Which made the séance into a murder case, impossible to ignore. And please remember there was an anonymous tip-off; a very timely one at that,' said Bartolli. 'The police arrived just at the right moment. Coincidence? Hardly.'

'And Lapointe found the link that pulled all the threads together,' said Jack, pointing to his notebook, 'rather convincingly, I thought. He identified a trial of a notorious Mafia boss in Paris, involving both the police officer in charge of the investigation and the presiding judge. Both attended the séance, opening the door to corruption: undue influence in the conduct and outcome of the trial. When Lapointe presented the evidence to his superiors, he was told that it was speculative, insufficient and inconclusive, especially without Cagliostro, who was also the main murder suspect, to provide a credible link to any involvement by the Mafia. Any suggestion of wrongdoing or corruption was dismissed.'

'Unbelievable,' said Bartolli. 'Yet in a way, it's all classic Mafia. We've seen it all before. Especially you, Jack, in Florence.'

'Echoes of *Ars Moriendi*,' said Tristan, 'which almost killed me. Same mysterious outdoor setting, masked participants, death and danger. All arranged by the Mafia and involving high rollers. That was all about gambling and money. This seems to have been about influencing a court case by corrupting officials in charge.'

'Quite so. No wonder Lapointe is so bitter about this, and keen to find Cagliostro, because if he does, that could be the missing link that would allow him to reopen the case, solve the murder, and vindicate himself.'

'So, this is all about finding Lafayette,' said Tristan, 'albeit for different reasons. We want to find him because he could lead us to the tattooed head we are looking for, and Lapointe wants to find him because he believes he's Cagliostro, who arranged that fateful séance in 2016 and was in some way involved in the murder of the young prostitute, orchestrated by the Mafia.'

'That just about sums it up,' said Dupree. 'And the matters Dr Garnier told us about could be useful in finding Lafayette; don't you think, Francesca?'

'Absolutely,' said Bartolli. 'As far as I'm concerned, those matters are the most interesting, and possibly the most useful information so far.'

'In what way?' said Jack.

'Because they could hold the key not only to finding Lafayette, but also leading us to Tristan's tattooed head.'

'How?' said Jack.

'Because they help us understand the criminal mind, which we can use to our advantage.'

'Really?' said Dupree. 'Just like you did with Landru and O'Hara?'

'Yes. When we take a closer look, criminals are actually quite predictable and follow a clear pattern of behaviour. It's all about reading the signs and interpreting them correctly.'

'And do you believe that you can do this by using what Dr Garnier told us about Lafayette to make this possible?' said Jack.

'Yes, I believe I can.'

'How exactly?'

'I'll tell you, but first, may I have another gin and tonic?'

'Coming up.'

Jack joined Dupree in the cottage kitchen for a nightcap after everyone else had gone to bed. 'Well, what do you think?' he asked and poured himself a cognac.

'About Francesca's assessment? The Lafayette profile?'

'Aha.'

'You know what I think about her. She was spot on about Landru, but no-one listened.'

'Until much later—'

'When you made contact with her and brought her back into the case.'

'And you think this is similar?'

'We must take what she said about Lafayette seriously,' said Dupree.

'I am.'

'Are you prepared to go along with what she suggested?'

'It's a great idea,' said Jack.

'That's not what I asked.'

'Yes, I am.'

'All the way?'

'Sure. Are you?'

'What do you think? It's a clever idea and our best bet to flush him out. Adrienne certainly seems to be on board. In fact, she loved the whole thing.'

'Looks that way,' said Jack. 'I was impressed by how Francesca took the various pieces of information Garnier provided from a psychological point of view, and turned them into a credible analysis to build a profile of a criminal.'

'And what exactly does that profile tell us about Lafayette, *the man*?'

'Well, let's have a look.' Jack reached for his drink and stared pensively into the glass in his hand as if it were a crystal ball that could reveal the future. 'If we accept what the Craigieburns have come up with about Lafayette's background, which I do, then we have a direct link between his grandmother Madame Lumière, and the tattooed head we're looking for.'

'Agreed.'

'This then brings us to this scandal and unsolved murder case in 2016 that Lapointe is so concerned about. If we accept the newspaper argument – speculative as it may be – that Lafayette and Cagliostro are the same person, then Lafayette, the psychiatric patient Garnier was talking about, is our man. Correct?'

'Yes, he is.'

'Then what kind of man are we talking about here?' asked Jack rhetorically. 'According to Francesca, who has used the information provided by Garnier to build a profile of Lafayette *the criminal*, we have the following: a man in his forties who, abandoned by his parents, grew up on the streets of Montmartre. We have no idea who his mother was, but his father, Joachim Lafayette, an alcoholic, died in some refuge while Lafayette was still a teenager. This was the beginning of a life of crime that has persisted to this very day.'

'Don't forget the influence Madame Lumière, his psychic grandmother, had on him,' Dupree reminded Jack.

'I'm coming to that. When Lafayette was about fourteen, his grandmother tracked him down and made contact with him. Lafayette went to live with her in Montmartre. This was how he came into contact with the occult, an obsession that has dominated his life ever since—'

'And which, according to Garnier, has resulted in some serious mental health problems over the years,' interjected Dupree, 'which have led to several admissions to Sainte-Anne's for treatment while he was in jail.'

'Correct. Depression and schizophrenia were considered the most serious chronic brain disorders, which manifested themselves in strange ways. Do you remember what Garnier told us about that?' asked Jack.

'Sure do. According to Garnier, Lafayette, the mental health patient, was a fascinating case. Highly intelligent and well-read, albeit without much formal education, he knew a lot about the occult. No, more than that; he was obsessed with it.'

'That's right. Apparently, he could quote Blavatsky, Agrippa, and Francis Bacon, by heart, and discuss complex passages from various books. Gurdjieff's *Beelzebub's Tales to His Grandson* was his favourite, remember?' said Jack.

'So much so, he identified himself with Beelzebub's grandson, Hassain. A crazy, delusional notion, but real in his troubled mind. Garnier thought that this was a link to Lafayette's grandmother, who had such a profound influence on him.'

'And then, of course, there was Cagliostro's talking head, which Garnier dismissed as a fantasy. But we know better, don't we?'

'Sure do. The head is real and played an important part in Lafayette's life, and featured in his séances over the years,' said Dupree. 'A treasured possession he's unlikely to have parted with.'

'But to me, the most interesting bit was Garnier's last assessment of Lafayette, ordered by the Parole Board just before his release a few weeks ago. Do you remember what Lapointe told us about that?' said Jack.

'I do. Because Lafayette's mental condition had significantly deteriorated and his hallucinations and delusions had become more frequent and pronounced, Garnier advised against releasing Lafayette and recommended more treatment. Why? Because he had become a danger not only to himself, but possibly to others as well. Especially women.'

'Exactly. This was ignored by the authorities and Lafayette is therefore somewhere out there right now,' said Jack.

'And what *we* have to do is find him.'

'And the best way to do that is to follow Francesca's plan. What do you think?'

'As I told you before, I'm in.'

'So am I. And remember what Tristan said about all that: find Lafayette and we find the tattooed head. For what it's worth, I think he's right.'

'I agree,' said Dupree.

Jack put down his glass and looked at Dupree. 'All right then. Let's do it,' he said. 'Let's start with your contacts in Montmartre. After all, you lived there for years. And let's not forget that Francesca thought it was very unlikely Lafayette would have gone to live anywhere else after his release. It's his home patch where he feels comfortable. And for someone mentally unstable, that's hugely important. Like a lifeline that makes the real world less threatening and easier to cope with.'

'Agreed. I'll call my contacts in the morning. Hopefully, they'll be sober by then. At least some of them.'

Bistro Au Revoir, Montmartre: 17 October

Jack turned into one of the sleazy backstreets just below the Basilique du Sacré-Coeur and looked up at the neon sign above the door to make sure he was in the right place. All he had were two names: Bistro Au Revoir, and Lucille, but Dupree's instructions had been quite specific: 'Find the girl, and you'll find Lafayette.'

Let's see if he's right, thought Jack and walked into the noisy, smoke-filled brasserie. Feeling out of place in the crowded room full of locals, mainly tradesmen having a drink after work, Jack made his way to the bar and ordered a beer. 'I'm looking for Lucille,' he said and handed the barman a large tip.

'That's her over there,' replied the barman with a knowing smile as he pointed to a young woman sitting at the far end of the bar. 'Better hurry. She's very popular.'

Slowly, Jack walked over to the woman – a striking blonde in an insanely short skirt, her makeup a little too theatrical, her hair dishevelled – and sat down on a bar stool next to her. 'Can I buy you a drink?' he said, feeling foolish about the clumsy, stereotypical approach.

'I already have one, thank you,' said the woman, a little annoyed, but eyeing Jack with interest, nevertheless. It had been a slow night, and he looked like someone with money.

'Your glass is almost empty.'

'Almost.'

'J'adore ...' said Jack, changing tack.

'What did you just say?'

'J'adore by Dior; you're wearing it.'

'My perfume. How did you know?'

Jack shrugged. He had a good nose for fragrances. Guessing ladies' perfumes was something he had perfected over the years and used many times to break the ice in awkward situations.

144

'Not bad,' said the woman, smiling. 'You're absolutely right. It's my favourite. I'll have that drink now, if it's still on offer. Gin and Dubonnet.'

'How interesting,' said Jack. 'Did you know that gin and Dubonnet was the English Queen Mother's favourite aperitif before lunch?'

'If you say so, Monsieur …?'

'Please call me Jack.'

'I'm Lucille. What can I do for you, Jack?' purred Lucille, beginning the carnal, sex-for-money routine.

'I'm after something that may surprise you.'

'Few things surprise me, believe me. So, just tell me.'

'I'm after a séance …'

'*Vraiment?* You *are* full of surprises, Jack. First the perfume, now this. What makes you think that I would be able to provide a séance?'

'Not you, but someone you know.'

'Who?'

'Jean-Baptiste Lafayette.'

Silence.

So far so good, thought Jack. She hadn't protested or denied knowing him.

'Who are you?' said Lucille.

'I'm a friend of Mademoiselle Darrieux, a writer. You may have heard of her?'

'Can't say I have.'

'She's quite well known here in Paris, especially in society circles. She runs an exclusive hotel, Chateau Kuragin, just out of town.'

Lucille shook her head. 'Look around you, Jack. I don't mix in society circles.'

'But Monsieur Lafayette does, or did until a few years ago. Quite often, in fact. He used to conduct séances that were well known and very popular in certain circles.'

'Why are you telling me all this?'

'Because I was hoping that you would be able to put me in touch with Monsieur Lafayette.'

'Why?'

'Because of a proposal I would like to put to him. A very lucrative one,' added Jack, lowering his voice.

'What kind of proposal?'

She's interested, thought Jack. Time to bait the hook and reel it in slowly.

'Mademoiselle Darrieux would like to engage him to perform one of his séances at the chateau for a very famous guest who stays at the chateau often, and has specifically asked for him.'

'Really? Can you tell me who that famous guest is?'

'Sure. Have you heard of Isis, the rock star?'

'What! Isis? Of course I have. Who hasn't? Isis has asked for Jean-Baptiste? *Sérieusement?*'

'Yes, she likes the exotic and the occult. Her performances are well known for that, and so are her songs. *Resurrection* was a global hit. The rising glass coffin …?'

'Yes, of course, I remember. And she's asked for a séance?'

'Yes. To be conducted at the chateau. For her and a group of friends. Very exclusive …'

'When?'

'No date has been set as yet. Early days. First, we have to find out if Monsieur Lafayette is available and would be interested?'

'I see …'

Jack reached into his pocket, pulled out a wad of banknotes – about a thousand euros – and put them discreetly next to Lucille's drink.

'What's this?' asked Lucille.

'I've already taken up a lot of your valuable time. This is for you. If you can help me get in touch with Monsieur Lafayette, there will be more …'

'I'll see what I can do,' said Lucille and put her hand on Jack's knee. 'In the meantime, could I perhaps interest you in something that may surprise *you?*'

'Touché,' said Jack, laughing. 'Very tempting, but I do prefer the supernatural.'

'I don't believe you. Regardless, come back tomorrow, same time, and we'll see.'

'Excellent,' said Jack and stood up. 'I'll be there. Love your perfume. *Au Revoir.*'

'In case you change your mind, you know where to find me,' purred Lucille, giving Jack a coquettish look, and quickly slipped the money into her handbag.

Bistro Au Revoir: the next day, 18 October

'This is it,' said Jack and held the door open for Bartolli. 'Crunch time.'

'What a dump.'

'Don't knock it. It could hold all the answers we're looking for.'

'True. Let's see if you're right.'

Lucille was seated in her usual spot at the far end of the bar and looked up when Jack walked in.

'Drink?' said Jack.

'Why not? I could certainly do with one.'

'Champagne?'

'Sure. The barman will love you. I see you brought a friend?'

'Yes. This is Francesca. She would help organise the séance we discussed yesterday. Should it go ahead, that is.'

Jack walked over to the barman and ordered a bottle of champagne.

'Can he guess your perfume as well?' said Lucille, admiring Bartolli's beautiful, curly, honey-blonde hair, which obviously didn't need bottle enhancement like her own.

'He's very good at it,' said Bartolli, a little taken aback by the unexpected question. 'Quite unusual for a man, don't you think?'

'Sure is. Definitely a first for me, and I've seen all kinds of men, as you can imagine. But then, it's not my perfume they are interested in.'

Lucille reached for her handbag, pulled out a packet of Gauloises, offered Bartolli one, which she declined, and then lit up. Enjoying the nicotine rush, she watched Jack approach with an ice bucket and three glasses, which he lined up on the bar.

'Well, are we going to toast the future, or will this be a farewell drink?' he said as he opened the bottle.

'What do you think, Francesca?' said Lucille, watching Bartolli through the cigarette smoke curling lazily towards the colourful bottles behind the bar.

'The future, I think.'

'What makes you say that?'

'You.'

Me? In what way?'

'Your composed, relaxed confidence tells me that you're looking into the future. A farewell is something quite different. Always a little tense, sad perhaps, certainly backward-looking. Rarely relaxed,' said Bartolli.

'Very observant of you. I'm impressed. And what do *you* think, Jack?'

'I'm with Francesca,' said Jack and poured the champagne. 'But then, I am the wrong man to ask. We should really ask Jean-Baptiste Lafayette—'

'Why don't you? He's just behind you.'

Surprised, Jack spun around and almost bumped into a tall man standing directly behind him, a cold shiver racing down his spine as he looked into the man's piercing eyes. They reminded him of the Wizard: same penetrating gaze; same captivating, hypnotic pull; same warning of imminent danger. However, the rest of the man's handsome face, with its dashing moustache, reminded Jack of D'Artagnan, one of Alexandre Dumas' three musketeers, on an errand for Cardinal Richelieu. The only thing missing was the wide-brimmed musketeer hat with its iconic feather.

'Drink?' asked Jack, recovering quickly.

'Sure.'

Jack handed Lafayette his glass. 'Here, have mine. We were about to drink to the future. Can we count you in?'

'Perhaps.'

What a captivating man, Bartolli thought, watching Lafayette with interest while Lucille made the introductions. No wonder women were drawn to him; he was almost too good-looking.

Knowing the effect he had on women, Lafayette took a step towards Francesca.

'There are journey people, and there are destination people,' he said softly, his melodious voice seductive. 'I'm a journeyman who listens to the lessons of the past, keeps a firm eye on the destination, but enjoys the journey.' Lafayette paused and looked into Bartolli's eyes, his gaze unsettling. 'I wonder, which are you?'

'The past is just a memory, the future but an expectation; the only thing real is the present,' said Bartolli, well aware Lafayette was playing a game and testing the waters to help him decide which way to turn. It all fitted a pattern she had seen many times before in habitual criminals.

Lafayette turned towards Jack standing next to him. 'Then, why are we drinking to the future?'

'Because the best is yet to come,' said Jack, filling a glass he'd obtained from the bar.

'Is that what *you* believe?'

'I do.'

'In that case, why don't we drink to that and see if you're right?'

'Fine by me,' said Jack and lifted his glass. 'The best is yet to come,' he said. *'Santé!'*

'Now, why don't you tell me why you are so interested in a séance,' said Lafayette and looked expectantly at Bartolli.

Two hours and three bottles of champagne later, Jack and Bartolli settled into the comfortable back seat of the old Bentley on their way back to the chateau.

'You should have seen Lafayette's face when François pulled up in front of "the dump", as you called it,' said Jack.

'It gave everything we told him credibility. Bentleys have that kind of effect, especially chauffeur-driven ones.'

'I'm so glad I brought you along. The way you handled him was brilliant.'

'He's a complex character, that's for sure.'

'For a moment there, I thought it was touch and go,' said Jack.

'When you raised the question of the tattooed head?'

'Yes. That obviously touched a sensitive nerve, but we had to raise it. You can see why. At least now we know he still has the head, even after all these years, just as we thought. He virtually admitted it, and we made it clear that it had to be part of the séance because Isis had specifically asked for it.'

'It was the right thing to do. We had to be sure; I can see that.'

'So, what do you think got us over the line?' said Jack.

'Isis, money. And one more thing ...'

'I thought that too. To have someone like Isis ask about him and the talking head played to Lafayette's ego. And there's certainly a lot of ego involved here, don't you think?'

'Absolutely. Criminals like Lafayette are all driven by ego. They live in another world.'

Bartolli was going to mention Anielka, but decided not to because she knew it would open old wounds, especially as Lapointe had referred to her as well in connection with mental illness. Despite everything she had done and what she was, or perhaps because of it, Jack had been very fond of Anielka right up to her tragic end, which had affected him deeply.

'Can you believe that we agreed on an eye-watering fee of fifty-thousand euros for the night? Crazy, don't you think? You should have seen Lucille's eyes when we talked about it. They were almost popping out. To them, this is an astronomical sum,' said Jack.

'Small change in the scheme of things,' said Bartolli, 'when a billionaire rock star like Isis is involved. It made everything we told them believable, and our offer irresistible.'

'You're right. You said there was one more thing. Apart from Isis and money that got us over the line?'

'Yes. *You.*'

'Me? In what way?'

'Your inside knowledge about the occult. I had no idea that you were so familiar with the subject. Lafayette was certainly impressed, and he was able to shine because you knew what he was talking about. Ego, again.'

'You mean *Beelzebub's Tales to His Grandson?*'

'Few people would have known what that was all about or have even heard of Gurdjieff. Yet there you were, discussing Gurdjieff's epic like an expert. It raised the whole séance proposal to a different level. You really sounded like one of the initiated.'

'If you say so.'

'"*I bury the bone so deep that the dogs have to scratch for it.*" What a wonderful quote.'

'Classic Gurdjieff. Don't forget that Lafayette fancies himself as some kind of reincarnation of Beelzebub's grandson.'

'Be that as it may, when you break it all down, it's textbook schizophrenia,' said Bartolli.

'As I said, I'm glad you came along. I don't think I could have pulled this off without you. You saw him exactly for what he is, and played to his insecurities and ego. You challenged him to show us what he could do and gave him a stage – a big one: *Isis* – he couldn't possibly refuse.'

'And giving him such a big cash advance was smart. Despite the obvious risks. Money talks. Especially in this case. Let's not forget he has only recently been released from jail. He must be living off Lucille's earnings.'

'Which effectively makes him a pimp,' said Jack.

'Which he won't like, I can tell you. He's used to being in control, especially with women. Not depending on them for his next meal.'

'Makes sense.'

'So, how do you see the way forward?' asked Bartolli.

'Well, in a way, it's now all up to Darrieux and Isis. Adrienne will have to make the chateau available for us so that we can set the stage for the séance, so to speak. Isis and her occult-crazy friends eager to meet Lafayette and his talking head – and that includes us, by the way – will do the rest. Isis will love it.'

'She sure will.'

'I thought of leaving the arrangements for the séance evening up to Isis. She's a genius when it comes to creating shows with specific themes. Her concerts are legendary, especially the ones I attended in Mexico City – and in Muscat earlier this year. Absolutely breathtaking. All based on her ideas, right down to the costumes and the lighting, to create the right atmosphere and mood. I do not doubt that our evening will be a memorable event if we leave it all to her.'

'We should do that. Who shall we invite?' asked Bartolli.

'Family and close friends only, who know what this is all about. Definitely no outsiders. Let's not forget that we are doing this for Tristan.'

'What about Lapointe and his unsolved murder case?'

Jack shrugged. 'That's now part of it, whether we like it or not. A bit messy but we can't do anything about it except go along with it and hope that Lapointe can make some progress. He seems to be really counting on us.'

'Can you blame him? You've helped him before. Quite spectacularly so. Landru and the O'Hara affair?'

'True. And do you think he's hoping that this will somehow play out the same way?'

'I'm sure he is. After all, you delivered what law enforcement agencies throughout Europe had been working on for years and couldn't.'

'O'Hara?'

'Exactly. You are a victim of your own success, Jack.'

'Speaking of Lapointe, have you formed a view about Lafayette, alias Cagliostro, as a possible murder suspect?'

'Early days, but from what I've seen so far, I don't think his profile fits. Frankly, I don't think he did the killing. He was obviously there, and quite possibly knows who did it, but I don't think he was the one who slit that poor woman's throat. That's just not him. But all that is a matter for Lapointe.'

'It is, and the tattooed head is at the centre of it all. For us, of course, but also for Lapointe and his investigation. Dupree told me that Lapointe is confident that he can provide a credible link between Lafayette and Cagliostro, and place him at the crime scene. All he needs is the mummified head we're all after.'

'How will he do that? After all these years?'

'Not sure, but Dupree said that Lapointe has some kind of forensic evidence. DNA, perhaps. All Forensics need is access to the head.'

'Interesting.' Bartolli snuggled up to Jack and put her cheek against his shoulder. 'You sure have the knack.'

'The knack for what?'

'Finding enthralling cases to solve.'

'Aren't you forgetting something?'

'What?'

'I don't find these cases, they find *me*.'

'Because you're an adventure magnet? Is that it?'

'It's a hidden talent incorrigible rascals have. But don't tell anyone.'

'Ah. Is that what it is? I should have known …'

Moments later, Jack noticed Bartolli had fallen asleep. She only woke up when they crossed the little bridge over the moat leading to the chateau.

Time Machine Studios, London: 20 October

Isis sat in front of her computer in her study and stared at the MRI report she had received earlier that day. *It's definitely back,* she thought, trying in vain to control the icy needle of fear stabbing at her heart as the shadow of mortality threatened to overwhelm her. 'Nonsense! Greenberg thinks otherwise,' she muttered, trying to stay rational and positive, but the little demons of doubt wouldn't go away. What if he was wrong? Then she remembered what Tristan had said*: 'It's nothing; her body told me. Just now when she gave me a hug.'*

Feeling better, Isis was about to turn off the computer, when Lola walked in.

'You're not looking at it again, surely? *Enough!'* Lola reached across the desk and turned off the computer. 'Greenberg thinks it's nothing, and we are going over to Boston to see him in a couple of weeks. He didn't say it was urgent. That should tell you something, and remember what Tristan said.'

'He knows better, do you think?'

'For what it's worth, I do. He can hear the whis—'

'You're right.'

'Now, have you given some thought to what Jack suggested?' Lola knew the best way to deal with Isis when she was in one of her moods was to keep her busy. And the best way to keep her busy was to ignite the spark of creativity, which was never too far away and just waiting for an opportunity to burst forth and shine.

'The tattooed head séance? I have. What an extraordinary idea. Classic Jack, wouldn't you say?'

'It's certainly a clever way to flush out Lafayette. Make him bring the head to us rather than pursue him, and risk him going to ground and disappearing altogether. And you, my dear, are at the very centre of this entire exercise,' said Lola.

'You think so?'

'You heard what Jack said. It was only because of you that Lafayette agreed to perform the séance in the first place. In short, *you* are the main drawcard here. The main attraction. That's why Jack asked you to come up with some ideas for the evening. He knows what you can do, and so do I. Remember Mexico City? The crystal skull on top of the Aztec pyramid with a hundred thousand mesmerised fans cheering at the bottom? That was something. All your ideas.'

'You're right again,' said Isis, a hesitant smile spreading across her drawn face as she remembered that unforgettable concert, the memories lifting her slowly out of her gloomy mood. 'What I have in mind for the evening is this: we need a theme. I was thinking of the Day of the Dead—'

'As in the Mexican *Día de los Muertos*?'

'Precisely. What gave me the idea was the date Jack suggested for the séance: 2 November. The Day of the Dead. My grandmother Dolores always used to celebrate this day, remember?'

'Sure do. What a great idea!' said Lola.

'We could put on a fantastic show at the chateau, and the tattooed head would fit in perfectly as the centrepiece. After all, the séance is all about making contact with the dead.'

'Brilliant! We've got less than two weeks to get ready, you know.'

'That's enough. We have all the contacts we need. We'll treat this as a mini-concert performance. We know exactly how many will attend and who they are. We know them all. That helps with the costumes I have in mind. Perhaps masks, as well,' said Isis, becoming quite excited. She pulled a notepad across her desk, picked up a pencil, and began to sketch.

'Jack suggested the wine cellar as the venue for the séance, but we'll have the entire chateau at our disposal. Darrieux has already arranged everything,' said Lola.

'You can always rely on Adrienne. Excellent! The wine cellar is the perfect choice. I propose we create an Aztec temple burial scene.'

'As we did in Mexico with the glass coffin?'

'Exactly.'

'Better get on with it, then.'

'What do you think I'm doing?' said Isis.

'Let me know who you want to see tomorrow. I'll make the calls in the morning.'

'We'll start with the costumes. I'll be able to use some of mine we've used previously. An Aztec theme should fit in perfectly. After all, there is plenty of evidence that pre-Colombian festivities honouring the dead existed well before the Catholic Church introduced the Day of the Dead in Mexico, which was nothing more than a continuation of Aztec traditions.'

'You're absolutely right. The costume you wore for the Mexico City concert was breathtaking.'

'You really think so?'

'It was even featured in *Vogue*, remember?'

'Hm. I'll think about it. But for now, I better get stuck into this. I'm bursting with ideas!'

'I can see that,' said Lola, smiling, and quietly withdrew.

Kuragin chateau, before the séance: 2 November

10:00 am

After being stuck in the chaotic Paris morning traffic, François had just made it in time to meet Jack's flight from Venice.

'All right. You always know exactly what's going on, and we've been kept intentionally in the dark here. This has to change. *Now!*' said Jack, helping François put the luggage into the boot. 'Curiosity is killing us.'

'Exactly. We want to know what's happening,' said the countess.

'We're your friends, François,' Tristan chimed in, 'you can tell us.'

'I've been sworn to secrecy,' said François. 'You know what Mademoiselle Darrieux is like. Crossing her would have dire consequences.'

'He's got a point,' said Tristan, enjoying the man's obvious between-a-rock-and-a-hard-place discomfort.

'*Nonsense!* We won't tell,' said the countess.

'No way! She would know. Nothing gets past her. It's uncanny.'

'All right. Tell us what you can, then,' said Jack, holding a rear passenger door open for the countess.

'Isis arrived a couple of days ago with Lola and Boris, and took charge …'

'Charge of what?' asked the countess.

'The arrangements for tonight's séance.'

'It took this long?' asked Tristan.

'Oh, yes. Deliveries came all the way from London. Truckloads of it. Time Machine stuff from Isis's concert tours.'

'What kind of stuff?'

'Oh no!' said François. 'I can see what you are doing.'

'This is ridiculous,' said Jack. 'We are getting nowhere.'

'All I can tell you is that this will be a night to remember. I haven't seen preparations like this at the chateau before. Ever. You'd think we are putting on some opera or rock concert. You won't recognise the wine cellar …'

'What about Lafayette?' asked Jack, changing direction.

'Darrieux has been liaising with him, just as you asked. I am picking him up this afternoon.'

At least he hasn't done a runner, thought Jack, feeling a little more relaxed. Just as Francesca had said, money obviously talks. He needed them more than they needed him. Things seemed to be under control. Since he had asked Isis to assist with the séance arrangements two weeks earlier, Isis and Darrieux had taken over and kept Jack and Tristan out of it. It was going to be a surprise, they said, and had sent them home to Venice, and Bartolli had returned to Rome.

'Has Francesca arrived?' asked Tristan.

'Yes, last night.'

'And the Craigieburns?' said Jack.

'Due this afternoon.'

'And Lapointe?'

'Last I heard he was with Dupree in the cottage, making preparations.'

'Preparations for what?' asked the countess.

'You'll have to ask him that.'

'What else can you tell us?' asked Jack.

'It's all going to be a big surprise, that's really all I can tell you—'

'But that's not all you *know*?' Jack interjected.

François shrugged. 'Crossing Darrieux is one thing. Crossing Darrieux *and* Isis, well. I want to stay in one piece and keep my job.'

'Let's leave it,' said Tristan softly. 'We'll see Parema Te Pahau's head tonight. That *I* can tell you. For now, that's good enough for me.'

'All right. Keep your eyes on the road, François,' said the countess.

'Yes, Comtesse,' replied François, grateful for getting off so lightly.

* * *

12:00 pm

Jack pointed ahead as they were crossing the little bridge over the moat. Several vans were parked in front of the chateau and tradesmen were busily working on something that looked like floodlights on poles facing the entrance.

'What's going on here?' he asked.

'Those must be the laser light show people,' said François.

'You're kidding,' said Tristan.

'No. It's amazing. I saw some of it last night. It will transform the entire façade of the chateau into an … I'm already telling you too much,' said François and pulled up in front of the chateau.

Even before the countess could get out of the car, Isis appeared at the entrance and came slowly down the stairs to greet them, like a diva approaching the microphone at the Grammys.

'Welcome to *Día de los Muertos*, my friends,' said Isis, looking stunning in her multi-coloured bodysuit encrusted with glass beads, and feathers accentuating a helmet-shaped headdress that looked like a bird with a huge beak.

'You look like an Aztec goddess,' said Jack, giving Isis a hug. 'I can see you've been busy.'

'I promised Tristan a spectacle worthy of a famous ancestor,' said Isis, adjusting her heavy helmet. 'And there's no better day to make his acquaintance than today, the Day of the Dead. We will invite his soul to visit us and we'll do that with flowers, the *flor de muerto*. They should arrive any moment.'

'Flowers? What kind of flowers?' asked Tristan, who had overheard the remark.

'Marigolds. A Mexican tradition. It is believed that the scent and vivid colours of the petals will attract the soul and guide it to the family members waiting for it.'

'A nice thought,' said the countess, smiling. 'Let's hope it works.'

'May I suggest that you go to your rooms to freshen up?' said Isis. 'You will find your costumes in there. Festivities start at seven pm in the foyer. Cook has prepared some lunch for you and set a table in the kitchen.'

'Costumes? How exciting,' said the countess and followed François up the stairs to the entrance, feeling a little strange being a guest in her own chateau.

Isis turned to one of the tradesmen standing on top of a ladder adjusting a floodlight. '*Not like that*, George!' she shouted. Looking a little awkward in her high heels and ignoring the helmet, which had slipped off her head, she strutted over to the ladder and began giving instructions.

After a quick sandwich in the kitchen, Jack went straight to the Gatekeeper's Cottage to talk to Dupree and settle into his room. He had decided to stay with Dupree in the cottage rather than take a room in the chateau with the others.

'I was told I'd find you here,' said Jack as he walked into the cottage.

Lapointe stood up and shook hands with Jack. Bartolli gave him a peck on the cheek, and Dupree pointed to a chair. 'Perfect timing, as usual,' he said. 'Come and join us. We were just talking about you.'

'Strategy meeting?' said Jack. 'Or is it a war council?'

'A bit of both. Well, this is the day,' said Dupree, 'to catch a culprit we've been after for a long time—'

'And possibly solve a murder case that has been troubling me for years,' interjected Lapointe. 'And all thanks to you and Tristan.'

'Strange how a few small coincidences and trivial pieces in this complex puzzle have fallen into place to bring us to this point,' said Jack. 'All the way from New Zealand.'

'Nothing unusual about that,' said Bartolli. 'In fact, it all fits. It's always the little things that trip up the villains and eventually show us the way.'

'From what I've seen so far, there's nothing little about the preparations for this evening. Mademoiselle Darrieux and Isis are turning this into quite an event. Costumes, masks, laser lights, and who knows what else ...'

Lapointe reached for his pipe. 'Not such a bad thing,' he said. 'It gives us a chance to blend in, participate, and wait for the right moment.'

'The right moment for what, exactly?' asked Jack.

'Lafayette will be in his element,' said Bartolli, sidestepping the question. 'If we are right and he and Cagliostro are the same person, he will follow the same modus operandi as he did on the night of the murder. He won't be able to help himself. And that includes the tattooed head you're after. He will use it in the performance, just as you requested.'

'And Claude and I will be right there in the audience,' said Lapointe, 'in disguise to observe it all, and two of my officers will be right here in the cottage to help us apprehend Lafayette. If everything goes to plan, that is.'

'And what plan is that?' asked Jack.

'Wait and see,' said Lapointe and lit his pipe.

'You obviously have something up your sleeve,' said Jack. 'So, we'll just go and enjoy the show, and see what happens? Is that it?'

'Always the best way,' said Bartolli.

'You are obviously in on all this.'

'Perhaps.'

'Are you going to tell me?'

'It's a fluid situation. Best left that way. To be authentic, certain things have to be spontaneous,' came the cryptic reply, 'not rehearsed.'

Jack shrugged. 'Okay. If you say so, Professor. How's Biscotti?'

'Last time I looked, he was sunning himself on his bed on the terrace. Mum's spoiling him rotten.'

'As expected.'

'Exactly. She's dotty about him.'

'In your professional opinion, what do you think will happen tonight? Will Tristan finally get his hands on the head of his ancestor, and will the Chief Superintendent here apprehend his suspect and finally solve the case that has given him so much grief over the years?'

Bartolli took her time before replying. 'Yes to both,' she said after a while. 'If we play our cards right.'

'That's good enough for me. Now, if you will excuse me, I need a quick shower,' said Jack, 'before I go with François to collect Lafayette in Montmartre.'

'To make sure that the star of the show makes an appearance?' teased Bartolli.

'That's obviously part of it, because without him there won't be a show and we cannot delve into the spirit world, leaving many of us red-faced and disappointed with no cards to play.'

'Don't worry, Jack. He's coming,' said Bartolli. 'He wouldn't miss this for the world.'

'I hope you're right.'

* * *

4:00 pm

Jack pointed ahead. 'There they are,' he said, relieved, as the Bentley pulled up in front of the bistro. François nodded and stopped the car.

Lafayette looked impressive in a black suit and white shirt with lace frills at the collar and cuffs, and Lucille was respectable in a skirt of reasonable length and a blouse that revealed enough to tease, but no more.

'Could we meet Isis before the séance, do you think?' asked Lafayette, putting some gear into the boot.

'I will arrange it,' said Jack. 'Do you have the head?' he said, watching Lafayette out of the corner of his eye. 'Isis asked me about it again this morning.'

Lafayette nodded and pointed to the rosewood box with the leather straps he had just put into the boot.

'All set, then. I think you will be impressed with the arrangements.'

'Mademoiselle Darrieux has kept us informed,' said Lucille, unable to hide her excitement. To her, this was the opportunity of a lifetime, and her ticket out of Montmartre.

'Isis has supervised everything personally. It's her party and her show, put on for her close friends. Very exclusive.'

This is the life, thought Lafayette, letting himself sink into the comfortable back seat. During the past week, he had carefully researched not only Isis and the Time Machine, but also Countess Kuragin and her chateau, and especially Mademoiselle Darrieux and her social circle, to get a 'feel' for the clientele attending the séance. This would help him deal with questions from the audience directed to departed loved ones, which was one of the main drawcards of the séance.

Normally, he would arrange a tarot card reading by his assistant before the séance, to gather helpful personal information he could use later during the séance, to great effect. But, of course, it was not possible on this occasion. Research on the Net was the next best thing to help him gather intelligence, which would allow him to improvise in a meaningful way when the time came to address questions from the audience directed to the departed through the medium. This was all part of a carefully prepared act Lafayette had perfected over the years, based on subtle deception with help from gullible participants eager to believe, to turn the illusion into reality.

While Lafayette had promised Lucille a new life, he had no intention of taking her with him. He had a different plan. He would use the money from this windfall for a new start, which did not include Lucille. Lafayette had plans to go to Marseilles to link up with some contacts he had made in jail who were in the lucrative drug business, and leave the squalor of Montmartre – and Lucille – behind for good. All he needed was one last successful performance, and he intended to make it a memorable one.

* * *

7:00 pm

Jack looked at Dupree and Lapointe, standing at the cottage door, and gasped.

'Few would believe that we are looking at Detective Chief Superintendent Lapointe over there, don't you think, Claude?'

Wearing a black T-shirt embossed with a white skeleton, beneath a black cape with a high, stiff collar that reminded Jack of Count Dracula, Lapointe looked like someone who had stepped straight out of a vintage horror movie.

'No comment, but you should take a look at yourself, Jack. We're all wearing the same.'

'Point taken,' replied Jack, laughing. 'At least we don't have to put on our masks just yet. I understand that's for later.'

'Adrienne dropped in several times already to make sure that we were ready and properly attired. Being late could have dire consequences. We better go.'

'How was Lafayette?' asked Lapointe as they were walking towards the chateau, which was lit up like a stage with fingers of coloured lights exploring the façade.

'Excited, confident, in his element. Just as Francesca predicted.'

'Good. That may even make dressing up worthwhile. What do you think, Claude?'

'No comment,' said Dupree, shaking his head. 'The things we do to catch villains.'

'At least on this occasion, we may even have a little fun along the way, gentlemen,' said Jack. 'Can you hear the music?'

'Sure. Sounds Mexican?' said Lapointe.

'It is. Mariachi, I'd say. Isis has chosen a Mexican theme for the night: *Día de los Muertos* – The Day of the Dead. Most appropriate, wouldn't you say?'

'No doubt about Isis. She knows how to put on a show,' said Dupree.

'Oh, yes, she can do that. She knows how to wow a hundred thousand screaming fans. I've seen her do it. And Adrienne will make sure that all of us play our part. Look, here she comes now,' said Jack and pointed to the entrance.

'Hurry up!' said Darrieux, looking formidable in her Aztec-inspired costume borrowed from Isis, bristling with feathers that even after rigorous, some would say ruthless, alteration was still several sizes too small; the consequences eye-popping. 'Everyone's already inside. Come and join the party.'

The opulent foyer of the chateau had been transformed into a gateway leading into the ruins of an ancient Aztec temple somewhere in the middle of the jungle. Black drapes covered the walls, and all furniture had been removed and replaced by realistic, massive tree trunks made of cardboard.

However, the most striking special effects came from clever images – mainly human skulls and ferocious-looking Aztec gods covered in blood – projected by laser lights against the drapes and the intricate marble stairs. This was clever projection mapping, giving the impression of massive stone blocks held together by tree roots leading to the back of the foyer, which now looked like the entrance into another, mysterious world of bloodthirsty gods, violent death and human sacrifice.

Lola walked up to Jack as soon as he entered.

'I've been trying to see you all day,' she said. 'We have to talk.'

'Is there a problem?'

'No. As you can see, this has turned into a much bigger project than we originally envisaged.'

'You can say that again,' said Jack, watching the Mariachi band walk around the foyer in their big sombreros and traditional attire. 'Lafayette and his assistant were certainly impressed. Where are they now?'

'Getting ready. Downstairs, in the wine-tasting room. We are keeping them away from the guests.'

'Good idea. Anyone keeping an eye on them?'

'Yes. Boris.'

Jack nodded. 'Excellent. And besides, there's really nowhere to go from down there except to come up here.'

'This has been very good for Isis,' said Lola, lowering her voice. 'Almost therapeutic. That's what I wanted to tell you. The tumour scare …'

'Oh? I thought she was over that. At least for now.'

'More test results, I'm afraid.'

'Bad ones?'

Lola shrugged. 'We're seeing Greenberg in Boston next week. Until then, this is the perfect distraction. Darrieux knows about this and was very supportive. They make a good team.'

'I bet. They would both be finalists in a competition for the most outrageous, in various categories.'

'No harm done. We are in for quite a night, as you'll see. Isis has spent a small fortune on this and rehearsed for hours. She's reliving her glory days.' Lola pointed to the top of the stairs. 'Look, here she comes now.'

Another well-timed entrance, no doubt, thought Jack, well aware of what was likely to come. He had experienced it many times before, but nothing could have prepared him for the spectacle about to unfold.

As soon as Isis appeared at the top of the stairs, the Mariachi band stopped playing, the silence that followed potent and full of anticipation. Then suddenly, the lights dimmed and the sound system crackled into life with a heart-stopping drum solo, introducing *Resurrection,* Isis's mega-hit that had taken the world by storm. When the guitars joined in, a beam of blue light moved slowly up the stairs and came to rest on Isis, standing motionless at the top landing like an apparition.

Dressed head-to-toe in a skin-tight black bodysuit with a printed outline of a white skeleton following the contours of her athletic body right down to her fingertips and toes, Isis looked like a moving skeleton, floating slowly down the stairs, her face hidden behind a mask of a grinning skull staring sightlessly into space.

So realistic was the scene that it made the fine hairs on the back of Jack's neck tingle with anticipation.

Wow! That's really something, he thought, mesmerised, as he watched Isis move her head and hands, pretending to sing as *Resurrection* boomed through the speakers, the chilling lyrics speaking of the finality of death and the eternal hope of resurrection.

As soon as the song came to an end, the lights went out, plunging the foyer into total darkness. A few moments later, a new beam of light appeared at the top of the stairs, accompanied by another stirring drum solo, and began to drift slowly down – step by step – until it reached the very spot where Isis, just moments before, had been swallowed up by darkness.

'*Watch,*' said Lola, and squeezed Jack's arm as a silhouette appeared and took shape. The eerie white skeleton had vanished, and so had the mask of the grinning skull, replaced by a figure in a stunning leopard-skin bodysuit, and makeup that gave Isis's expressive face a distinctly feline look.

'Welcome to *Día de los Muertos*, my friends, where anything is possible and only limited by your imagination,' said Isis, coming slowly down the remaining stairs, the atmosphere in the transformed foyer electric as spontaneous cheering and applause erupted from below.

'How on earth did she do that?' said Jack.

'This is straight out of one of her concerts in Buenos Aires, which gave her the nickname *El Maga*, magician in Spanish. She's rehearsed the costume change for days,' said Lola.

'What; the skeleton just peels off?'

'Something like that.'

'Amazing. Back from the dead?'

'Let's hope so. Come and give her a hug. She could do with it,' said Lola and walked over to Isis standing at the bottom of the stairs, basking in the adulation of her excited friends surrounding her.

Tristan was one of the first to embrace Isis. 'Thank you,' he said. 'I can't tell you what this means to me.'

'And to me.'

'I know. You've surrounded yourself with death, but there's nothing to be afraid of because this isn't your time.'

'How do you know?'

'I can't explain it; I just do.'

'That should be enough for now,' said Jack, patting Isis on the back. 'You look absolutely stunning. Definitely in the world of the living; wouldn't you agree, Tristan?'

'Absolutely. Choosing *Día de los Muertos* as the theme for the occasion was genius.'

'There are more surprises to come,' said Isis, feeling her spirits lifting.

'I can't wait,' said Tristan.

'Nor can I. Now, let's have some food.' Jack pointed to the platters of food being offered by waiters. 'Just look at that!'

'Mexican food. Very authentic,' said Isis, laughing. 'You and food, Jack. I can almost believe what people say behind your back.'

'What's that?'

'They call you a bottomless larrikin-pit when it comes to food,' said Lola, who had overheard the question.

'*Seriously?* What do you have to say about this, Tristan?' asked Jack, raising an eyebrow.

'No comment. Try one of these. They look delicious.'

'Tamales. Traditional Mexican food. Cornmeal dough filled with minced meat and red peppers. I'm sure you'll like it,' said Isis, taking one from a passing waiter. 'Delicious! I'm starving. Haven't eaten all day.'

'I know why,' said Lola.

'Why?' asked Isis, munching happily.

'So that you can fit into this—'

'Enough! Not another word, you hear?'

Lola rolled her eyes. 'As you wish, but don't expect me to be your food police when it suits you.'

'I don't know what you mean. Now, let's enjoy some food and a couple of drinks before the main event. What do you think, Jack?'

'Great idea. I think I'll have another tamale.'

The séance: 8:00 pm

An hour later, Darrieux invited everyone to put on their white skull masks, as the main event of the evening was about to begin. The Mariachi ensemble playing *ranchera* had put away their traditional instruments, and the *vihuela* and *guitarrón* were replaced by pan flutes and drums, giving the music a distinctly ethereal sound of the Andes. All carefully choreographed and chosen by Isis, who knew the subtle influence of music played a crucial part in creating a suitable mood and atmosphere that would define the highlight of the evening.

With the musicians leading the way, the guests followed Darrieux and Isis down the stairs into the wine cellar. Black drapes covering the wine racks and bottles, and clever lighting effects, had transformed the cellar into an Aztec burial chamber deep inside the imaginary jungle pyramid created in the foyer above.

'Not bad,' said Jack, linking arms with Bartolli. 'What do you think?'

'Clever in many ways. Not only will this entertain the guests, but it will also draw out Lafayette and tempt him to reveal his true self, and perhaps even give away something about the murder. Ego and bravado; classic signs of this type of criminal mind. After all, that's what Lapointe and Claude are hoping for, right?'

'Correct. As long as we get our hands on the *Mokomokai*, that's what really matters here. The rest is just a bonus.'

At the back of the wine cellar, Lafayette was putting the finishing touches to the props he would use for his act. As he heard the music, he knew it was almost time.

'Now, you know what to do?' he said and positioned the Houdini box, as he called it, exactly where he wanted it to be: directly at the front, in clear view of the spectators.

'Absolutely!' said Lucille, looking sexy in her black fishnet stockings, high heels and tiny gold bikini, accentuating her long legs and shapely figure.

'Getting into the box quickly is crucial. After that, you just wait for my signal and do exactly as I showed you. Understood?'

'Yes. Just as we've rehearsed. It's simple.'

'That's the beauty of this act. It's simple and the effect is stunning, just like you, *chérie*,' said Lafayette and gave Lucille a peck on the cheek.

'I had no idea you were so clever. This act is brilliant!'

'I've used it many times in the past. Quickly! Get into position. Here they come now.'

The space at the far end of the cellar had been slightly raised to create a stage with what looked like some kind of sacrificial Aztec altar made of wood, which Isis had used in one of her acts before. Dozens of candles created an air of mystery, casting crazy shadows against the drapes, like dancing demons watching. It was the perfect setting for a magic act relying on sleight of hand, misdirection, audience management, and a carefully rehearsed performance using specific props designed to influence imagination and make-believe.

Boris, who would act as Lafayette's assistant, stepped behind a curtain to get out of sight, and Lafayette moved into the background with Lucille, waiting for the spectators to be seated and let the anticipation grow.

Wearing a black cape over his black suit, white gloves, a black top hat and a striking white latex skull mask, Lafayette walked slowly into the circle of light at the edge of the stage.

'Welcome to *Día de los Muertos*, ladies and gentlemen, where anything is possible and only limited by your imagination,' he said and turned around to face Lucille, who walked slowly forwards out of the shadows until she stood next to him in her rather skimpy but eye-catching attire. This was quite intentional, as Lafayette wanted her to be the focus of attention, allowing him to stay in the background, which was all part of the act.

'Tonight, we shall invite a restless spirit to join us on this Day of the Dead,' began Lafayette after he had introduced Lucille as Esmeralda. 'A spirit who has waited a long time to meet the one person who can bring it peace.' Lafayette paused and looked around the room.

'And that person, ladies and gentlemen, is among us right here tonight. Not only will this restless spirit join us, but it will do this in a way that may surprise, even shock many of you. How? I hear you ask. Well, let me show you.'

Lafayette turned towards a trunk the size of a small suitcase, and pointed to it. 'It's all about an exchange. Esmeralda, in exchange for the spirit. Esmeralda will step into this trunk here and travel to the spirit world, to make it possible for the restless spirit to join us. She will remain there for as long as the spirit decides to stay with us in the here and now. Esmeralda, are you ready?' asked Lafayette with a flourish.

Lucille walked over to the trunk and opened its lid. 'I am,' she replied and climbed into the trunk, which was barely big enough to accommodate her in a kneeling position. She lowered her head and slowly closed the lid from inside.

Bending down, Lafayette placed both his hands on the lid like a healer, and kept staring intently at the spectators watching him. Then slowly, he withdrew his hands and turned around to face the back of the stage. 'Boris, could you please come and help me?' he asked. Moments later, the black curtain at the back parted, and Boris, stripped to the waist, stepped out from behind, his huge, powerful wrestler frame radiating raw strength. Wearing a white skull mask just like Lafayette, he walked over to the trunk and, holding it by its two handles, lifted it up for all to see, before placing it carefully on top of the altar. Then, taking a bow, he returned slowly to the back and disappeared behind the curtain.

'Now, I need a volunteer,' said Lafayette, pointing to the mesmerised audience watching his every move. 'Perhaps the young man who can "hear the whisper of angels and glimpse eternity" would like to step forward and assist the restless spirit that has been waiting such a long time to meet him?'

Jack turned to Tristan sitting next to him. 'I think that's you, my friend,' he said. 'Better go and help.'

'How on earth does he know all this?' hissed Tristan and stood up.

'It's an old trick and what's coming next is older still, and has been done before – by Houdini.'

'Ah. Here he comes, ladies and gentlemen. Please step up here and stand next to the trunk,' said Lafayette and moved into the shadows.

Tristan walked up on stage and did as he was told, his black cape and skull mask looking quite surreal. 'Now, please open the lid.'

Feeling suddenly dizzy, Tristan opened the lid – his heart beating like a drum – looked inside, and gasped. Lucille had disappeared. The trunk was empty except for a tattooed human head on a red cushion at the bottom, staring at him with sightless eyes from beyond the grave. Tristan let go of the lid as if bitten by a snake and stepped back, almost losing his balance.

'What do you see; can you tell us?' asked Lafayette, his voice sounding otherworldly as he walked over to the trunk while Tristan rushed back to his seat. 'I'm sure everyone here would like to know. Here, let me help you.'

With that, Lafayette opened the lid and as he did so, the front panel of the trunk disengaged and fell forward, exposing the mummified head inside for all to see.

A ripple of excitement washed over the spectators as the impact of the surprise revelation hit its mark and the implications of the stunning act began to sink in.

Cybil squeezed her husband's hand. '*We did it!*' she whispered.

'Thanks mainly to you,' replied Richard, squeezing her hand in response.

Feeling calm and in control, Lapointe turned to Dupree sitting next to him. 'Everything in place?' he whispered.

'Yes. The officers are upstairs, waiting for our signal.'

'Good. Let's see how deep a hole this rogue can dig for himself before we take him away.'

Jack looked at Bartolli. 'What's next, do you think?' he whispered. 'Watch.'

'Now, ladies and gentlemen, while the spirit is with us, we must use the time wisely. If you would like to ask the spirit a question –

173

perhaps about a departed loved one? – this is the time,' said Lafayette, holding out his cape like the wings of a bat as he hovered above the open trunk like a magician.

'I have a question,' said Isis and stood up.

'Please go ahead,' replied Lafayette and walked backwards into the shadows at the back of the stage, leaving the open trunk with the head in the spotlight.

'How much time do I have in the here and now, before I too, will join the spirit world?' asked Isis, her voice sounding hoarse as she gazed at the grotesque head in the trunk.

Suddenly, a green, fog-like substance began to ooze out of the head's nostrils.

'Look! Ectoplasm, just like Eva Carrière,' said Cybil, as the green fog began to rise and obscure the nose and mouth of the head.

'That's clever, don't you think?' said Darrieux to Lola, sitting next to her at the back.

'I wish she hadn't asked the question,' replied Lola, frowning.

'Life is full of uncertainties,' said a deep voice that in no way sounded like Lafayette, 'and time can be capricious.' It was impossible to tell where it was coming from. 'As an artist, you know that better than most. When I part the curtain of the future, I cannot see you, which means that your arrival in the spirit world is not imminent.'

Obviously relieved, Isis nodded and sat down.

'I too have a question,' said Lapointe and stood up.

Here it comes, thought Jack, recognising Lapointe's distinctive voice.

'My question is directed to the spirit of Monique, a young woman who was killed on 16 October 2016, not far from here, during a séance not unlike this one.'

Lapointe paused to let this sink in, the silence in the chamber so potent, a needle falling onto the stone floor would have startled the audience. Because Lafayette was obscured, standing in the shadows, it was impossible to gauge his reaction to the loaded question.

'Who was the one who slit your throat?' continued Lapointe after a while. 'Was it Cagliostro, standing right here in front of us now, or was it someone else?'

Momentarily frozen, Lafayette kept staring straight ahead, refusing to believe what he had just heard. But when he saw two uniformed police officers enter the chamber, the spell was broken. As a habitual criminal who had been arrested countless times, he knew exactly what was happening: his cover blown, he was about to be taken into custody.

I don't believe this! he thought, his mind racing, and looked at Lucille crouching under the makeshift altar in front of him, ready for the signal to climb back into the trunk when the time was right. *I can't go back to jail!*

When he reached into his pocket and felt the cold steel of the flick-knife he always carried with him, a possible way out began to take shape in his feverish mind, replacing the desperation of a cornered animal, with the cunning daring of someone who had nothing to lose. Bending down, Lafayette grabbed Lucille by the hair. 'Get up!' he shouted and pulled her roughly towards him.

Before the officers could make it to the stage, Lafayette was holding the razor-sharp blade to Lucille's throat. 'Stop where you are!' he shouted, 'Or she dies. Her life is in your hands.'

'Stop!' ordered Lapointe, well aware desperate people do desperate things, and Lafayette wouldn't hesitate to carry out the threat.

'This is what will happen now,' said Lafayette. 'Everyone stays exactly where they are. François will bring the car around, and Lucille and I will walk out of here and get into the car.'

He's got balls, thought Jack.

'If anyone makes a move, she dies. If anyone follows us, she dies. If we are stopped along the way, she dies. Am I making myself clear?'

'Absolutely,' said Lapointe and took off his mask. 'You got it.'

'Are you police?'

'Yes, I am. Detective Chief Superintendent Marcel Lapointe, Senior Commissaire of the Paris Brigade Criminelle.'

Lafayette shook his head in disbelief, finding it difficult to come to terms with the position he found himself in. 'I hope you're enjoying the show, because it's far from over,' said Lafayette and began to push Lucille slowly forward, the knife almost touching her throat.

As he walked past the open trunk, a large hand shot out from behind the curtain, grabbed him by the wrist and twisted the hand with the knife away from Lucille's throat. Screaming, Lucille fell to the floor. Moments later, Boris appeared and put his free arm around Lafayette from behind, his grip vice-like. Taken completely by surprise, Lafayette tried to free himself from Boris's grip, but couldn't. However, he did have the presence of mind to grab the knife with his free hand instead of dropping it. Unable to turn around, he began to stab at Boris's hand and arm, hoping to loosen the grip, but Boris wouldn't let go. By now, blood was gushing out of deep wounds, but still, Boris wouldn't let go. Ignoring the pain, he tightened his grip even further, like a wrestler sensing victory.

By now, the two police officers had jumped on the stage and were trying to subdue Lafayette, who was resisting violently. Shouting instructions, Lapointe and Dupree joined them and helped pin down Lafayette on the floor.

Isis and Lola ran up to Boris, holding his bleeding arm – blood dripping onto the slippery floor – the chaos and shouting in the chamber deafening as everyone tried to do something to help.

Having witnessed many serious injuries during his time as a war correspondent in Afghanistan, Jack knew exactly what to do. The flow of blood had to be stemmed. Looking around for something suitable, his eyes came to rest on one of the black drapes. He pulled one off the wine rack, picked up the flick-knife lying on the floor, and began to tear strips of material off the curtain with the tip of the knife. Then he walked over to Boris. 'Hold still, my friend,' he said, 'we'll have you fixed up in a jiffy.'

'It's nothing,' said Boris, a broad smile on his face as Jack began to wind strips of material around the injured hand and arm.

'You're supposed to protect *me*, you silly man,' reprimanded Isis, relieved to see Boris out of danger, 'not strangers.'

'Sorry.'

'I didn't quite expect this,' said Bartolli, 'but I'm not surprised. Can I help?'

'Sure. Tie this here into a knot. Make it tight,' said Jack.

'I've never met an incorrigible rascal who was also good at first aid.'

'Always a first time. Necessity is a good teacher and I'm an attentive pupil.'

'In the classroom of life?' said Bartolli, tying the knot.

'Something like that. This should do it!'

'Ambulance is on its way,' said Dupree.

'He'll live, but more importantly, he will be able to play the balalaika again once this heals,' said Jack.

'Thanks Jack,' said Boris, grinning. 'What is this Aussie saying you keep using all the time? Your blood's—'

'Worth bottling,' said Tristan, completing the sentence. 'But don't you lose any more. The bottle is full already.'

* * *

11:00 pm

Drained and exhausted, everyone had gone into the music room to calm down and relax after the turbulent events of the evening. Accompanied by Isis and Lola, Boris had been taken to hospital, and Lapointe had gone with the police officers back to Paris to interrogate Lafayette and Lucille. Dupree was talking with the Craigieburns, and Darrieux was sitting by herself in front of the fireplace with a brandy balloon in her hand and looking somewhat forlorn.

'Where's Tristan?' asked the countess.

'I left him downstairs,' said Jack.

'With the tattooed head of his ancestor? *Alone?*'

'Yes.'

'But that was more than an hour ago. Let's go and see him.'

'Good idea.'

The countess stopped at the bottom of the stairs leading down into the wine cellar and pointed ahead.

'There he is. Look,' she said.

Most of the candles had gone out, leaving the chamber almost in darkness. Tristan was kneeling in front of the open trunk, motionless and silent, staring at the head of Parema Te Pahau.

'What do you think he's doing?'

'Communicating with a painful reminder of a violent past.'

Tristan looked up when he saw Jack and the countess approach. 'Even in death, there is violence all around him,' said Tristan. 'Lafayette was right. This is a restless spirit. We must take him home for burial. *Soon.*'

'That may have to wait a while,' said Jack.

'What do you mean?'

'I spoke to Lapointe just before he left. The head is now evidence in a murder case.'

'How come?'

'Apparently, a few strands of hair thought to belong to the *Mokomokai* were recovered at the murder scene, and if Lapointe is right, and this is the head that was present at that fateful séance seven years ago, then this is the evidence he needs to link Lafayette to the crime scene and reopen the case.'

'DNA?' asked the countess.

'Yes. For that reason, we cannot take the head with us now. And besides, there are other complications.'

'What kind of complications?' said Tristan.

'These are human remains of cultural importance, belonging to another country.'

'What are you telling me? We can't take the head back to New Zealand for burial? Is that what you're saying?'

'Yes. Not yet.'

'What do you mean?'

'Forensics only need a hair sample. That shouldn't take long. The other matters I mentioned are in a different category altogether and a little more complicated, but we can do something about that.'

'What?'

'Make an application under the New Zealand Karanga Aotearoa Repatriation Programme for the repatriation of Māori remains, as your grandmother mentioned. Lapointe thinks that is the best way forward, and he will support this all the way up to ministerial level until formal approval is a given. We just have to be patient and comply with all the legalities involved, and I know just the person who'll be able to help us do that.'

'My grandmother?'

'Who else?'

'Where does this leave us now?' said Tristan and stood up, looking concerned.

'We'll get there, trust me. We've come this far, and we are certainly not stopping now. Everyone's behind you,' said Jack and put his hand on Tristan's shoulder.

Tristan nodded. 'There's something I want to say. Right now. Here in front of my ancestor,' he said, becoming emotional.

'Go on,' prompted the countess.

'I may have lost my parents early in life, in circumstances too painful to remember but impossible to forget, but I've gained a family. You two are my family. You are my rock, my shelter from the storms raging in my heart – and my head, from time to time – and for that, I will be forever grateful,' said Tristan, his voice barely audible.

Slowly, the countess leaned forward and kissed Tristan tenderly on the forehead, the touch of her lips like a balm banishing the painful memories. 'You know you are like a son to me, and nothing will ever change that,' whispered the countess, her eyes moist with tears.

When Tristan turned towards Jack standing next to him and looked into his eyes, he smiled because he realised he was looking into his friend's soul. 'Nothing to say, Jack?'

'No need. You already know all I want to say, don't you?'

'Love and friendship?'

'What else?'

Kyoto: Four months later

'Will someone please tell me why we're flying to Kyoto first?' said Tristan.

'It's a surprise,' said Isis, playing chess with Jack at the back of the plane. Lola was still at the controls in the cockpit with the two co-pilots. After leaving Venice, she had announced a detour: they were on their way to Japan, not New Zealand. No explanation followed.

'Obviously, something to do with the Kennin-ji Temple?' said Tristan.

'Obviously,' said Isis. 'Good move, Jack. Reminds me of the game between Byrne and Fischer in 1956.'

'The Game of the Century?' Jack shook his head. 'No wonder; I rarely win.'

'Just try a little harder.'

'Just because Greenberg gave you a clean bill of health, there's no need to be so cocky.'

'I told her there was nothing to worry about, didn't I?' said Tristan. 'But no-one listened. Sandwich, anyone?'

'Good idea,' said Jack, 'I'm starving, and I'm losing again anyway.'

'Food to the rescue?' said Isis. 'Three moves to checkmate; watch.'

'I don't know why I bother.'

'Don't worry, you're getting better.'

'Really? Doesn't feel that way.'

'It takes time.'

'If you say so.'

'You have other talents, Jack,' said Tristan.

'Such as?'

'You know how to charm people and gain their trust. Getting export approval for our *Mokomokai* in record time is a good example.'

'That was Lapointe and Dupree's doing.'

'No, it wasn't. You took the minister – a lady, by the way – to lunch at La Closerie des Lilas, of all places, and it all went from there.'

'That's true,' said Isis, 'I heard about that. Adrienne told me. You know how to charm women, Jack. We all know that.'

'And does that include you?'

'Sometimes.'

'Obviously not when playing chess.'

Isis shrugged and put away the chess set. 'It's a long flight. I think I'll take a nap.'

'Beauty sleep before we meet the abbot?' teased Jack.

'I don't need sleep to look my best,' said Isis in a huff, and walked to the back of the plane. 'Tell Lola to wake me when we're almost there. I think I'll wear a kimono, or at least something Japanese-inspired,' she mumbled and closed the door to her private cabin behind her.

Lola had arranged a hire car to meet them at Kansai International Airport and take them straight to the Kennin-ji Temple. It was just after sunrise, and the tourists hadn't arrived yet.

'So, why exactly are we here?' asked Tristan as he followed Jack to the entrance.

'Wait and see,' said Isis, looking stunning in her customised, tea ceremony-inspired dress: a vintage jacquard *qipao* – a long *cheongsam* with faux gambiered silk fabric. 'I always wanted to see this place. Remember, Lola? We never had the time after the concerts in Tokyo.'

'We're here now.'

'Look, there he is,' said Jack and pointed to the entrance.

Ikkyu and two monks were waiting on the inside of the impressive gate. One of the monks unlocked the gate and opened it.

'Welcome,' said Ikkyu and shook hands with Jack.

'I believe congratulations are in order. You are the new abbot.'

'I am indeed. The responsibilities were passed to me by Abbot Tetsudo Moro, who died peacefully three weeks ago. Moro sama will be a hard act to follow. And this must be Isis?' said Abbot Ikkyu. 'What an honour. We spoke on the phone.'

'Several times. The honour is all mine,' replied Isis and bowed.

'Let's go into the Dharma Hall. Everything is ready, just as you requested.'

Tristan had remained in the background and was watching with interest.

'You obviously had a hand in this,' he said, turning to Jack. 'What's going on?'

'Wait and see,' said Jack and followed Abbot Ikkyu inside.

Isis looked up at the ceiling as soon as they entered the magnificent Dharma Hall, one of the great attractions of the temple. 'That's really something,' she said. 'You weren't exaggerating when you told me about the twin dragons.'

'So, how would you like us to do this?' said Abbot Ikkyu. 'I understand this is supposed to be a surprise for the young man standing over there.' The abbot pointed to Tristan.

'It is. Perhaps if we could see it first?' said Jack.

'Certainly.' Abbot Ikkyu spoke to one of the monks, who then left the hall.

He returned moments later carrying what looked like an ornate, rectangular, lacquered box, placed it carefully on a small table next to an incense burner, and stepped away.

Isis looked at Tristan standing in the shadows, watching her.

'Why don't you open this for us, Tristan? I'm sure you know what's inside.'

Slowly, Tristan walked up to the table without taking his eyes off the box, a feeling of calmness washing over him. 'Another moment of destiny,' he said. 'I know what's inside, but none of us have seen it before. Not the real thing …'

'Open it,' said Jack.

Taking a deep breath, Tristan lifted the lid and looked inside, an expression of surprise and wonder spreading across his face as he looked at Goldie's stunning portrait of Parema Te Pahau. While Goldie may have used the mummified head of the dead warrior chief years after his death as inspiration, he had managed to capture him on canvas so vividly, that to Tristan he appeared momentarily alive, looking at him like a proud father finally being reunited with a long-lost son.

'M-magnificent,' stammered Tristan, tears welling in his eyes. 'It's so beautiful and so lifelike.'

'And it's yours,' said Isis.

Tristan turned around and looked at Isis. 'What do you mean?'

'It's yours; that's what it means.'

'Jack, I don't understand—'

'Isis bought it for you. We thought it would be a shame for this painting to remain here, hidden in this monastery, perhaps forever. And the late Abbot Tetsudo Moro agreed. I kept in touch with him as he requested, and told him how we found the tattooed head and what that meant to you.'

Jack paused and looked at Tristan. 'The painting belongs to you now,' he continued. 'Since the Bone Scraper's death, you are the last of your line, and you should take it back home to New Zealand with Parema Te Pahau's head. The head for burial; the portrait to remember him by as he was.'

'I-I don't know what to say,' Tristan stammered again.

'There's no need to say anything,' said Isis. 'For now, why don't you take the painting back to the plane, put it next to the head, and we'll continue our journey to the Chatham Islands. What do you think, Jack?'

'Sounds like a plan. I know someone who is anxiously waiting for our arrival.'

'Who?'

'Kiri Te Papatahi, Tristan's grandmother. She's expecting Te Pahau's head for burial, of course, but not the Goldie portrait. That will be a huge surprise.'

'Someone once told me that we are but temporary custodians of other men's genius,' said Tristan. 'Could that have been you perhaps, Jack?'

'Who knows? But it's true.'

'It is,' said Abbot Ikkyu, smiling. 'Abbot Tetsudo Moro used to say something very similar and he always looked at art in that way. Art transcends time and people, and ownership as we know it has no

183

meaning. The painting is going home to where it belongs, and we are just instruments of fate to make that possible.'

'How true. We are indebted to you, Abbot sama,' said Isis. 'I believe destiny has brought us together here this morning in this spiritual place, but we must leave now and complete our journey.'

'I understand,' said Abbot Ikkyu. 'And thank you for your generous donation to our monastery.'

'Not only are we temporary custodians of other men's genius,' said Isis, 'I believe the same applies to money. All we can hope to do is spend it wisely ... while we can,' she added, as she remembered the relief she had felt when Dr Greenberg had assured her the tumour hadn't returned.

'Well said, but thank you, nevertheless.'

Tristan looked up at the ceiling and let his eyes glide over Koizumi Junsaku's stunning masterpiece for the last time. Then he picked up the lacquered box and turned towards Abbot Ikkyu, watching him.

'From now on, I will no longer walk alone and hear the sound of one hand clapping, because Abbot Tetsudo Moro has answered my call for help. May the Dharma Rain descend on this place, bring new life and enlightenment to all, and offer liberation from suffering.'

With that, Tristan made a bow and carried the lacquered box slowly towards the shaft of sunlight reaching through the open doors like a beacon of hope.

Afterword

The return of Parema Te Pahau's head to Waitangi became a nationwide celebration of Māori culture. All thanks to the Karanga Aotearoa Repatriation Programme for the repatriation of Māori remains, championed by Tristan's grandmother.

The traditional burial of the remains was televised nationwide and Tristan's speech unravelling the *Mokomokai*'s astonishing tale and the pivotal role played by Goldie's portrait of the warrior chief, captivated global audiences.

During the burial speech, Tristan made an announcement that received worldwide press coverage and was even mentioned in the New Zealand parliament. Tristan's bold decision to gift Goldie's painting to the Auckland Art Gallery sparked international discourse, declaring: 'It belongs to the people of New Zealand, not temporary custodians of other men's genius.'

This inspirational quote made headlines throughout New Zealand and beyond, and ignited serious discussion and debate about the repatriation of human remains and artworks held in museums and galleries around the world.

* * *

After extensive questioning that lasted for days, Lafayette admitted he was present at the 2016 séance and had officiated as 'Cagliostro', but denied any involvement in the murder of his assistant, Monique. To exonerate himself, he provided helpful information – including names – that implicated the Mafia and allowed Lapointe to reopen the case.

Based on the available evidence, Lapointe decided it was highly unlikely Lafayette did the killing, and that the murder was carried out by a hired Mafia assassin to put further pressure on the judge and the high-ranking police officer present at the séance.

After numerous tests and careful examination under hypnosis, the prosecutor accepted Dr Garnier's recommendation that Lafayette was mentally unfit to stand trial, and should instead be admitted to the Sainte-Anne Hospital Centre for treatment.

Lucille was released without charge and used the money received for her part in the séance at the Kuragin chateau, to leave Montmartre and start a new life.

* * *

During a brief stopover in Auckland on the way back to Europe, Tristan and Jack presented the Goldie painting to a speechless curator, who had heard about the intended gift only a few days earlier on TV.

At a hastily arranged ceremony held at the Auckland Art Gallery, which was also attended by the auctioneer Hamish McNamara and his sister, the curator thanked Tristan for his generous gift on behalf of a grateful nation, and made a promise.

As a reminder of the portrait's extraordinary journey, she promised to display Goldie's sketch of Parema Te Pahau's tattooed head next to the painting, together with a brief outline of the portrait's history, to remind visitors that ownership of true art has no meaning, *because we are but temporary custodians of other men's genius.*

More Books by the Author

In 2013, I released my first adventure thriller –
The Empress Holds the Key.

The Empress Holds the Key

A disturbing, edge-of-your-seat historical mystery thriller

Jack Rogan Mysteries Book 1

Dark secrets. A holy relic. An ancient quest reignited.
Amidst the charred remnants of a rustic Australian haven, journalist
Jack Rogan stumbles upon a haunting photograph - igniting a trail of
peril and intrigue of unparalleled proportions.

Journey through a labyrinth of startling revelations, from Nazi
treasures and covert Swiss vaults to the shadows of an old-world grave.
At its core? A sacred relic, lost in the sands of time, now beckoning to
those daring enough to seek it.

From the golden sands of ancient Egypt to the clandestine
corridors of the Knights Templar, Rogan finds himself in a race against
time, battling unseen forces. Will he unearth a secret that could rock
the very pillars of the Catholic Church, or will age-old truths remain
shrouded in eternal mystery?

Discover an adventure that melds heart-pounding escapades, rich history, and intricate plots. Dive into The Empress Holds the Key and experience Gabriel Farago's storytelling prowess firsthand.

The Empress Holds the Key
is now available in ebook and paperback

Encouraged by the reception of *The Empress Holds the Key*, I released my next thriller *–The Disappearance of Anna Popov –* in 2014.

The Disappearance of Anna Popov

A dark, page-turning psychological thriller

Jack Rogan Mysteries Book 2

A mysterious disappearance. An outlaw bikie gang. One dangerous investigation.

Journalist Jack Rogan cannot resist a good mystery. When he stumbles across a hidden clue about the tragic disappearance of two girls from Alice Springs years earlier, he's determined to investigate.

Joining forces with his New York literary agent; a retired Aboriginal police officer; and Cassandra, an enigmatic psychic, Rogan enters the dark and dangerous world of an outlaw bikie gang ruled by an evil master.

Entangled in a web of violence, superstition and fear, Rogan and his friends follow the trail of the missing girls into the remote Dream-time-wilderness of Outback Australia, where they face their greatest challenge yet.

Cassandra has a secret agenda of her own and uses her occult powers to conjure up an epic showdown where the stakes are high, and the loser faces death and oblivion.

Will Rogan succeed in finding the truth, or will the forces of evil prevail, causing untold misery and destroying even more lives?

**Gold Medal Winner in Psychological Mysteries
– Thriller Category**
The Global Book Awards 2022

The Disappearance of Anna Popov
is now available in ebook and paperback

My next book, *The Hidden Genes of Professor K*, was released in 2016.

The Hidden Genes of Professor K

A dark, disturbing and nail-biting medical thriller

Jack Rogan Mysteries Book 3

A medical breakthrough. A greedy pharmaceutical magnate. A brutal double-murder. One tangled web of lies.
World-renowned scientist Professor K is close to a ground-breaking discovery. He's also dying. With his last breath, he anoints Dr Alexandra Delacroix as his successor and pleads with her to carry on his work.

But powerful forces will stop at nothing to possess the research, unwittingly plunging Delacroix into a treacherous world of unbridled ambition and greed.

Desperate and alone, she turns to celebrated author and journalist Jack Rogan.

Rogan must help Delacroix, while also assisting famous rock star Isis in the seemingly unrelated investigation into the brutal murder of her parents.

With the support of Isis's resourceful PA, Lola; a former police officer; a tireless campaigner for the destitute and forgotten; and a gifted boy with psychic powers, Rogan exposes a complex web of fiercely guarded secrets and heinous crimes of the past that can ruin them all and change history.

Will the dreams of a visionary scientist with the power to change the future of medicine fall into the wrong hands, or will his genius benefit mankind and prevent untold misery and suffering for generations to come?

"Outstanding Thriller" of 2017
Independent Author Network Book of the Year Awards

The Hidden Genes of Professor K
is now available in ebook and paperback

My next book, *Professor K: The Final Quest*,
was released in October 2018.

Professor K: The Final Quest

An action-packed historical medical mystery

Jack Rogan Mysteries Book 4

A desperate plea from the Vatican. A kidnapped chef. An ambitious mob boss. One perilous game.

When Professor Alexandra Delacroix is called in to find a cure for the dying pope, she follows clues left by her mentor and friend, the late Professor K, which lead her on a breathtaking search through historical secrets, some of them deadly.

Her old friend Jack Rogan must step in to assist while also searching for kidnapped Top Chef Europe winner Lorenza da Baggio.

He joins forces with his young friend and gifted psychic, Tristan; a dedicated Mafia-hunting prosecutor; a fearless young police officer; and an enigmatic Egyptian detective who is on a perilous hunt for a notorious IS terrorist.

Together, they stand off with the head of a powerful Mafia family in Florence and uncover a network of corruption and heinous crimes reaching to the very top.

Will Rogan and his friends succeed in finding Lorenza and curing the pope, or will the dark forces swirling around them prevail in their sinister plots?

Gold Medal Winner in the Fiction – Thriller – Medical Category
Readers' Favorite 2019 International Book Awards Contest

Professor K: The Final Quest
is now available in ebook and paperback

My next book, *The Curious Case of the Missing Head*,
was released in November 2019.

The Curious Case of the Missing Head

A gripping medical thriller

Jack Rogan Mysteries Book 5

**A headless body on a boat. An international conspiracy. Can a
kidnapped genius survive a controversial scientific discovery?**

Esteemed Australian journalist Jack Rogan is on a mission to solve the
disappearance of his mother in the 1970s. But when a friend needs
help rescuing a kidnapped world-renowned astrophysicist, he doesn't
hesitate. Struggling with more questions than answers, his investigation
leads them aboard a hellish hospital ship, where instead of finding the
kidnap victim, he's confronted with a decapitated corpse.

As the search intensifies, Jack bumps up against diabolical cartels
with hidden agendas. And when his research reveals dubious experiments, a criminal on death row, and a shocking revelation about his
mother's fate, he must uncover how it's all linked.

Can Jack unravel the twisted connections and catch the scientist's killer, or will the next obituary published be his own?

**Gold Medal Winner in the Fiction
– Thriller – Conspiracy Category**
Readers' Favorite 2020 International Book Awards Contest

"Outstanding Thriller/Suspense" of 2020
Independent Author Network Book of the Year Awards

The Curious Case of the Missing Head
is now available in ebook and paperback

My sixth book, *The Lost Symphony*, was released in November 2020.

The Lost Symphony

A historical mystery thriller

Jack Rogan Mysteries Book 6

A murdered tsarina. A lost musical masterpiece. A stolen Russian icon. Can Jack honour a promise made a long time ago, and solve an age-old mystery?

When acclaimed Australian journalist and author Jack Rogan inherits an old music box with a curious letter hidden inside, he decides to investigate. As he delves deeper into a murky past of secrets and violence, he soon discovers he's not the only one interested in solving the puzzle.

Frieda Malenkova, a ruthless art dealer; and Victor Sokolov, a Russian billionaire with a dark past, will stop at nothing to achieve their dark desires and foil Jack's valiant struggle to uncover the truth.

Joining forces with Mademoiselle Darrieux, a flamboyant Paris socialite; and Claude Dupree, a retired French police officer, Jack enters a dangerous world of unbridled ambition, murder and greed that threatens to destroy him.

On a perilous journey that takes him deep into Russia, Jack follows a tortuous path of discovery, disappointment and betrayal that brings him face to face with his destiny.

Will Jack unravel the hidden clues left behind by a desperate empress? Can he save the precious legacy of a genius before it's too late, and return a holy icon revered by generations to where it belongs?

**Gold Medal Winner in the Fiction
– Mystery – Historical Category**
Readers' Favorite 2021 International Book Awards Contest

**Award-Winning Finalist in the Fiction:
Thriller/Adventure Category**
The 2021 International Book Awards

"Outstanding Mystery" of 2021 - Mystery Category Winner
Independent Author Network Book of the Year Awards

The Lost Symphony
is now available in ebook and paperback

My next book, *The Death Mask Murders*,
was released in December 2021.

The Death Mask Murders

A historical mystery crime thriller

Jack Rogan Mysteries Book 7

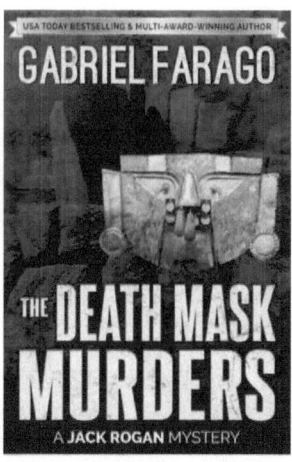

Seven brutal murders. A cursed Inca burial mask. A lost treasure. One deadly game.

When convicted killer Maurice Landru reaches out from a Paris prison and asks for help to prove his innocence, celebrated author Jack Rogan cannot resist. Drawn into a web of hidden clues pointing to an ancient mystery, Jack decides to investigate.

Joining forces with Francesca Bartolli, a glamorous criminal profiler; Mademoiselle Darrieux, an eccentric Paris socialite; and Claude Dupree, a retired French police officer, Jack enters a dangerous world of depraved cyber-gambling, where the stakes are high and the players will stop at nothing to satisfy their dark desires.

Following his 'breadcrumbs of destiny', Jack soon comes up against an evil genius who terminates his enemies without mercy and is prepared to risk all to win.

On a perilous journey littered with violence and death, Jack uncovers dark secrets of a murky past of ruthless conquistadors, bloodthirsty pirates and shipwrecked priests, all pointing to a fabulous treasure, waiting to be discovered.

Can Jack expose the mastermind behind the horrific murders and retrieve the legendary treasure before it falls into the wrong hands, or will the forces of darkness overwhelm him and destroy everything he believes in?

Gold Medal Winner in the Fiction
- Mystery - Historical Category
Readers' Favorite 2022 International Book Awards Contest

"Outstanding Mystery" of 2022 - Mystery Category Winner
Independent Author Network Book of the Year Awards

The Death Mask Murders
is now available in ebook and paperback

My latest book, *The Stolen Altarpiece*, was released in April 2023.

The Stolen Altarpiece

A historical mystery crime thriller
Jack Rogan Mysteries Book 8

A long-forgotten amulet. A stolen painting. A dark threat reignited. One deadly geopolitical power-play.
Jack Rogan's discovery of a hidden letter reaching out of the past unwittingly embarks the journalist into a perilous quest to find a holy relic that has the power to fight evil.

As he follows a web of intriguing clues that take him on a dangerous journey to the Middle East, Rogan soon crosses swords with an old adversary, who is determined to destroy him and those he holds dear.

Soon, secrets buried in a famous stolen painting point to Russia and the threat of war in Ukraine. Joining forces with Tristan, a gifted psychic; Abbot Serapion, a Russian monk; and Sasha, the daughter of a Russian billionaire, Jack enters a dangerous geopolitical arena ruled by a deranged, corrupt man consumed by unbridled ambition and lust for power, who threatens to enslave a nation and destroy an entire country to satisfy his misguided vision of greatness.

Can Jack find a way to defeat the dark forces of evil and turn the tide of history before it's too late, or will the horrors of war continue, and consume a people who dared to stand against tyranny and dream of freedom?

Gold Medal Winner in the Fiction - Thriller - Political Category
Readers' Favorite 2023 International Book Awards Contest

Gold Medal Winner in Amateur Sleuth - Thriller Category
The Global Book Awards 2023

"Outstanding Mystery" of 2023 - Mystery Category Winner
Independent Author Network Book of the Year Awards

"Outstanding Action/Adventure" of 2023
– Action/Adventure Category Winner
Independent Author Network Book of the Year Awards

"First Place: Fiction Book of the Year Winner' of 2023
Independent Author Network Book of the Year Awards

The Stolen Altarpiece
is now available in ebook and paperback

About the Author

Gabriel Farago is the *USA TODAY* best-selling and multi-award-winning Australian author of *The Jack Rogan Mysteries Series* for the thinking reader.

As a lawyer with a passion for history and archaeology, Gabriel Farago had to wait many years before being able to pursue another passion – writing – in earnest. However, his love of books and story-telling started long before that.

'I remember as a young boy reading biographies and history books with a torch under the bed covers,' he recalls, 'and then writing stories about archaeologists and explorers the next day, instead of doing homework. While I regularly got into trouble for this, I believe we can only do well in our endeavours if we are passionate about the things we love. For me, writing has become a passion.'

Born in Budapest, Gabriel grew up in postwar Europe and, after fleeing Hungary with his parents during the Revolution in 1956, he went to school in Austria before arriving in Australia as a teenager. This allowed him to become multilingual and feel 'at home' in different countries and diverse cultures.

Shaped by a long legal career and experiences spanning several decades and continents, his is a mature voice that speaks in many tongues. Gabriel holds degrees in literature and law, speaks several languages and takes research and authenticity very seriously. Inquisitive by nature, he studied Egyptology and learned to read the hieroglyphs. He travels extensively and visits all the locations mentioned in his books.

'I try to weave fact and fiction into a seamless storyline,' he explains. 'By blurring the boundaries between the two, the reader is never quite sure where one ends, and the other begins. This is, of course, quite deliberate, as it creates the illusion of authenticity and reality in a work that is pure fiction. A successful work of fiction is a balancing act: reality must rub shoulders with imagination in a way that is both entertaining and plausible.'

Gabriel lives just outside Sydney, Australia, in the Blue Mountains, surrounded by a World Heritage National Park. 'The beauty and solitude of this unique environment,' he points out, 'gives me the inspiration and energy to weave my thoughts and ideas into stories that in turn, I sincerely hope, will entertain and inspire my readers.'

Gabriel Farago

Author's Note

I hope you enjoyed reading this book as much as I enjoyed writing it. I'd be very grateful if you'd post a short review on Amazon. Your support really does make a difference.

Connect with the Author

Amazon
https://www.amazon.com/stores/
Gabriel-Farago/author/B00GUVY2UW

Website
https://gabrielfarago.com.au/

Goodreads
https://www.goodreads.com/author/show/7435911.Gabriel_Farago

Facebook
https://www.facebook.com/GabrielFaragoAuthor

BookBub
https://www.bookbub.com/profile/gabriel-farago

www.ingramcontent.com/pod-product-compliance
Lightning Source LLC
Chambersburg PA
CBHW051249250626
47155CB00009B/3223